HAUNTED CANADA 4

MORE TRUE TALES OF TERROR

HAUNTED CANADA 4

MORE TRUE TALES OF TERROR

JOEL A. SUTHERLAND

Illustrations by
Norman Lanting

Scholastic Canada Ltd.
Toronto New York London Auckland Sydney
Mexico City New Delhi Hong Kong Buenos Aires

Scholastic Canada Ltd.
604 King Street West, Toronto, Ontario M5V 1E1, Canada

Scholastic Inc.
557 Broadway, New York, NY 10012, USA

Scholastic Australia Pty Limited
PO Box 579, Gosford, NSW 2250, Australia

Scholastic New Zealand Limited
Private Bag 94407, Botany, Manukau 2163, New Zealand

Scholastic Children's Books
Euston House, 24 Eversholt Street, London NW1 1DB, UK

www.scholastic.ca

Cover credits: Fotolia © davidevison (hood and skull);
Fotolia © lighthouse (hands reaching out of tunnel); Fotolia © davidevison (skull).
Illustrations by Norman Lanting.

Library and Archives Canada Cataloguing in Publication
Sutherland, Joel A., 1980-, author
Haunted Canada 4 : more true tales of terror / by Joel A.
Sutherland.

ISBN 978-1-4431-2893-3 (pbk.)

1. Ghosts--Canada--Juvenile literature. 2. Haunted places--
Canada--Juvenile literature. I. Title. II. Title: Haunted Canada four.

BF1472.C3S98 2014   j133.10971   C2013-907798-7

6 5 4 3 2 1   Printed in Canada 121   14 15 16 17 18

MIX
Paper from
responsible sources
FSC
www.fsc.org   FSC® C004071

For Charles, Bronwen and all the kids who believe, who want to believe and who will soon begin to believe . . .

PHOTO CREDITS

iNTRODUCTiON

Do you believe in ghosts? If so, welcome. Take a seat and prepare yourself for a night you'll never forget. A night of morbid curiosities, bloody murders and spirits from beyond the grave. A night of chills and thrills and goosebumps. A night of very little sleep.

If you don't believe in ghosts, give it time. Read a page or two. Ask yourself how it's possible that so many reputable and educated people have claimed to see spirits if they don't exist. How do so many ghost stories, reported by different people who have never met, match each other identically?

These reports pop up from coast to coast and in every corner of the country. Whether you live in British Columbia, Nunavut, Newfoundland and Labrador or any point in between, chances are there's a house around the corner from your own home that's haunted by spirits who simply can't rest in peace. And it's not only haunted houses you'll read about, either. No, ghosts have taken up permanent residence in hotels, hospitals, churches, the woods and even schools . . . Nowhere is safe.

Do I believe in ghosts? You better believe I do.

Read the stories that follow and I bet you'll begin to believe too.

One word of warning before you begin: if it's already late and the witching hour approaches, you might want to wait until morning before reading any further.

Frightfully Yours,

HORROR CINEMA VERITÉ

Coquitlam, British Columbia

The sound of footsteps on the second floor when you're alone in the house, an unfinished basement's locked trap door rattling on its hinges, a ghastly wail in the middle of the night — if you're a fan of scary movies, you're familiar with these cinematic clichés. Maybe you don't even jump when a shrieking cat leaps out of a dark corner, or when someone — or *something* — passes in front of the camera, unseen by the clueless characters on screen.

But for one actor with a small role in a horror movie filmed in an abandoned mental hospital, the biggest scares happened off-camera, and they weren't special effects. They were all too real. Riverview Hospital is home to a host of evil spirits that have plagued film crews working in the building for years. One of those spirits is particularly

1

vicious. It has razor-sharp teeth, a wicked bite and can run incredibly fast on all fours. Big dogs can be terrifying, but coming face to face with a *dead* dog? The horror movie actor will tell you that's much, much worse.

To understand where the negative energy within the abandoned mental hospital comes from, we need to go back to its beginning. In 1904 the province of British Columbia had a problem. The Provincial Asylum for the Insane in New Westminster was seriously overcrowded. With more than three hundred patients, children were forced to live side by side with potentially dangerous psychiatric patients. Reports started to surface of inadequate care, terrible hygiene and horrendous living conditions. A new, bigger building was needed, and it was needed right away.

The province purchased one thousand acres of land in 1904 and, in 1913, the Hospital for the Mind (later called Riverview Hospital) opened its doors in Coquitlam. It was considered to be on the cutting edge of psychiatric hospitals, but it wasn't long before the cracks started to appear — figuratively and literally. Electroshock therapy was used in an attempt to cure patients of their "insani-ty," as well as the highly controversial psychosurgery, or lobotomy, wherein a small piece of the brain is surgically removed. By 1951 there were nearly five thousand patients in Riverview Hospital, and serious overcrowding was once again a major concern.

The problem slowly corrected itself as the medical field shifted from favouring large mental hospitals to smaller buildings with fewer patients, and the population of Riverview gradually dwindled. In July 2012 it closed its doors for good.

Over the years the foreboding grandeur and general creepiness of the old buildings have made Riverview a beacon for film production companies. Many horror movies and television shows have been filmed in Riverview's dusty halls, making it the most filmed location in Canada.

But with such a powerful and long history of grief and pain etched into the hospital's walls, the scariest events have sometimes happened after the cameras stopped rolling.

Film crews working through the night have reported seeing former patients and staff suddenly appear and disappear. People have been shoved by unseen forces. The tunnels in the basement are said to be so full of negative energy that it's nearly impossible to enter them.

In 2004 an actor named Caz, quite possibly bored and most certainly brave, spent his nights exploring Riverview when he wasn't needed on set. The horror movie was being filmed in the West Lawn Building, which had been closed for more than twenty years.

In the infamous basement tunnels, he felt like he was being watched and sensed a bad presence. However, it was the fourth floor that turned Caz into a firm believer in ghosts.

It was after midnight. Caz stood alone at the end of a hallway that ran the length of the building. It was pitch-black other than the dim red light from an EXIT sign. He waited, rooted to the ground because he sensed . . . something.

Suddenly a dog charged at him from the far end of the hall. It was impossibly fast. And as it neared him, Caz noticed the beast was transparent. It lunged at him but, just before its teeth tore into his legs, the dog disappeared.

Caz didn't believe his own eyes, so he returned two more nights to see what would happen. Each night the phantom dog charged him, and each night it disappeared moments before knocking him down. Perhaps the phantom dog is charged with protecting the "Lady Bug Room," the fourth floor room where the majority of Riverview's paranormal activity takes place. The room received its unusual nickname in part because of the unexplained red dots, believed to be spirits, that often appear near the room in photographs.

The Lady Bug Room is odd, to say the least. Its door is the only one on the fourth floor that's locked. It's also the only door without a doorknob, making it impossible to enter. Finally, it's the only room in an otherwise uninhabited and powerless building with light streaming through the crack beneath the door.

What's inside the Lady Bug Room? No one really knows, but it's rumoured that an evil presence known as "The Candy Lady" dwells within. One thing known is that the fourth floor was at one time where the lobotomies were performed.

Caz couldn't resist the morbid desire to see what was in the Lady Bug Room. He returned one night and peered in through the keyhole. He pressed his ear against the door. He slowed his breathing and strained to hear something, anything. The hall became unnaturally quiet. And then he heard it, the sound from within the locked room in the abandoned mental hospital that sent him running as fast as his legs could carry him.

The sound of someone breathing.

The West Lawn Building, Riverview Hospital

Horror movies don't hold a candle to the real-life horrors found at the end of darkened hallways, in musty tunnels and behind locked doors.

ROTTING IN A CAGE

Lévis, Quebec

"There is scarcely any woman in all of Canadian history who has a worse reputation than Marie-Josephte Corriveau." So reads the opening sentence of Corriveau's entry in the *Dictionary of Canadian Biography*. In life, Marie-Josephte Corriveau was a beautiful woman, but in death she became something vile and heinous, a sickening reminder to the people of Lévis to obey the letter of the law.

Born in Saint-Vallier, Quebec, in 1733, she married her first husband, a farmer named Charles Bouchard, at the young age of sixteen. They had three children and remained together for eleven years despite whispered rumours that theirs was not a happy, peaceful union. The townsfolk believed that Charles was mean and abusive to his young wife. Marie-Josephte was miserable, and many

7

thought she might be better off on her own. Nevertheless, no one suspected the woman of any wrongdoing when Charles was found dead in 1760, nor did it seem strange that Marie-Josephte should remarry a mere fifteen months later. The times were tough and she had to put the well-being of her children first, assuring they'd have a roof over their heads and food to eat.

She married another farmer, Louis Etienne Dodier. All seemed well at first, but it wasn't long before cracks began to appear in their relationship and it would soon come to a deadly end. A mere year and a half after the wedding, Louis was found dead in his own stable. Marie-Josephte argued that their horse must have kicked and trampled her new husband — his head was caved in and his face covered in lacerations — but the locals were no longer so trusting of the young woman. An inquiry was launched by the British military authorities who had recently con-quered New France. It was quickly ruled that the horse played no part in Louis's death.

It was well known that Marie-Josephte's father, Joseph, did not approve of his daughter's second marriage and was on bad terms with Louis. The military tribunal found him guilty of the homicide and sentenced him to hang, while Marie-Josephte was found to be an accomplice and sen-tenced to sixty lashes and to be branded with the letter M on her hand.

Neither punishment was carried out. On the eve of his execution, Joseph finally admitted that he had wanted to protect his daughter from the hangman's noose and therefore hadn't proclaimed his own innocence, but in reality he had played no part in Louis's death. The guilt, he confessed with a heavy heart, lay entirely upon his daughter's shoulders.

A second trial began and Marie-Josephte testified to striking her husband twice on the head with an axe while he slept. She then dragged his body from the house to the horse stable to make the murder look like an accident. No one knows why she decided at this time to admit the truth. Perhaps her guilty conscience was too much to bear. Perhaps, like many serial killers, she craved attention. But with the admission of guilt came new speculation about the mysterious and sudden death of her first husband. And her legend has grown over the years to falsely claim she had as many as seven husbands, all of whom she murdered in gruesome fashions such as poisoning, strangulation and impalement with a pitchfork. It's even been said she boiled one of her husbands alive.

The charges against Joseph Corriveau were dropped and Marie-Josephte was sentenced to hang for her crimes. But that punishment alone would not be satisfactory for such an evil and treacherous person who some were now coming to believe was a sorceress with dark powers. After hanging, her corpse was ordered to be placed in an iron cage in the shape of a human body and strung up for public display.

The terrible act was carried out in 1763. Her cadaver was hung in the cage at a busy crossroads in the woods that would later become known as La Corriveau Forest. The cage — body and all — was left swaying in the wind for thirty-eight days to serve as a warning. Her skin blackened and peeled away from her bones. Her hair fell out, and animals picked at her flesh. The stench was atrocious. But as her body withered away, so did the belief that Marie-Josephte could no longer harm the living.

The eerie sounds of grinding metal and clattering bones kept most late-night travellers from venturing near the cursed intersection. Those who weren't superstitious or easily spooked, and passed the swaying cage, arrived at their destinations with pale faces and stories of the rotting body that had opened its eyes, lunged for them with decaying hands and whispered their name with a guttural voice. With every passing day, the stories grew wilder and more frightening. Marie-Josephte's body was finally moved to a nearby cemetery, but no one was brave enough to free it. Cage and Corriveau were buried together.

The townsfolk had hoped that'd be the last they'd hear of Marie-Josephte, but they were dead wrong. Not long after she had been buried, an upstanding young man named François Dubé was travelling home to his wife. When he passed the tree where the cage used to hang, he saw an odd vision across the river. Demonic figures danced wildly around the crackling flames of a blue fire. Just as François turned to flee, a pair of bony, slimy hands clutched his throat from behind and held him in place.

"Take me across the river, Dubé," the rotting corpse of Marie-Josephte hissed in his ear. "I cannot pass the blessed waters of the Saint Lawrence unless a Christian man carries me."

François fell to the ground as he tried to free himself from Marie-Josephte's supernaturally strong grasp. As he pulled at her arms, her maggot-ridden flesh ripped off her bones and wriggled in his hands. François finally succumbed to extreme fright and fainted in a heap on the side of the road. His wife found him there the next morning, nearly paralyzed with fear but thankful to still be alive.

Reports of the ghost of Marie-Josephte rising from her grave to torment passersby in La Corriveau Forest still creep up today. Those who remember her tale — and it's nearly impossible to forget — are wise to get off the roads, out of the woods and into the safety of their homes long before nightfall in the city of Lévis.

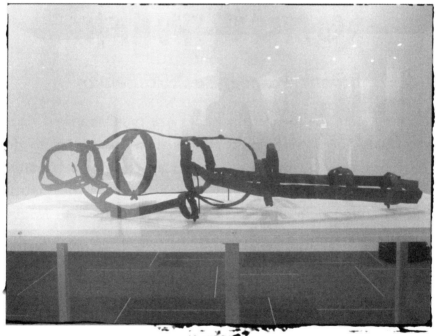

The cage that held Marie-Josephte Corriveau's body

RED EYES IN THE NIGHT

Roche Percée, Saskatchewan

Some ghosts are peaceful, others are mean-spirited. But regardless of their disposition, most seem unable to do much physical harm to the living. That couldn't be further from the truth when it comes to the rugeroos that haunt the abandoned Roche Percée mines. According to Native legends that date back hundreds of years, rugeroos are spirits with red eyes that cut through the dark. They are monstrously huge and can appear as a mix of man and animal, most commonly the coyote. And they guard their territory fiercely, attacking anyone who dares to venture too close.

Roche Percée is a small village southeast of the city of Estevan. Translated from French its name means "pierced rock," which is how the First Nations peoples who have camped in the area for many years describe the odd geological formation. The village grew in the 1880s when people discovered coal, which was dug out of the ground and transported to Winnipeg. The first large-scale coal mine was established in 1891. Within a few years there were dozens of mines in operation, and Roche Percée was a bustling community of miners and fortune-seekers. But by the 1950s most of the coal-mining companies had left, and in 2011 a massive flood forced many of the remaining residents to abandon their homes, leaving behind a ghost town of damaged buildings and empty mines.

The pierced rock also remains, a massive landmark of sandstone that juts up from the ground like a giant, bony hand from a grave. The wind blowing through its many holes, tunnels and crevices creates an eerie screech that has long been revered and feared by all who hear it. Those

Postcard of Roche Percée dated 1917

who are brave enough to enter the tunnels have felt compelled to inscribe their names on the rock walls, including General Custer and his famed U.S. 7th Cavalry in the 1800s.

Rugeroo sightings have been reported by tourists and locals for as long as Roche Percée has existed. The only sound they make is a low, menacing growl. And, if their target doesn't flee immediately, they attack. Those who are wise enough to retreat are followed by the spirit's disembodied red eyes through the woods far from the rugeroo's territory.

Reports of these spirits have varied, but each description is as terrifying as the last. Courtney Chistensen was once stalked by a rugeroo. It was a fat, furry creature, taller than a deer, part wolf and part bear. Jan Drummond described a rugeroo that was spotted walking on the roof of a school. It had the head and antlers of a deer and the legs of a man. Everyone swore that seeing it was a bad omen.

So if the sight of a giant half-man, half-beast ghost with glowing red eyes wasn't enough to send you running, now you know that it's also a bad omen — just in case you might've otherwise decided to stick around when a rugeroo confronts you in the woods.

THE HANGED MAN

Bridgetown, Nova Scotia

"The Prettiest Little Town in Nova Scotia" — that's the unofficial motto of Bridgetown (population 949), which was incorporated in 1897. Victorian houses line the streets, the small-town shops are huddled close together and people greet each other warmly on every street corner. An annual triathlon in the summer and a cider festival in the fall draw happy crowds. It's quiet and peaceful, and that's exactly how the townsfolk like it.

But then the townsfolk aren't the ones spending their evenings at the Stem ta Stern Bed and Breakfast. They aren't the ones who have discovered Bridgetown nights can be anything but quiet and peaceful. They aren't the ones huddled under their bedsheets, listening to the hollow *rat-a-tat-tat* of bony fingers upon their windows.

The Stem ta Stern is a Queen Anne revival home with two guest rooms. Much of its period architecture has been preserved, including the stained glass, the front turret and the original wood throughout. Bridgetown was once a vital shipbuilding town with plenty of wealth, and the beautiful homes reflect this heritage. They also have the perfect look for a movie about a haunted house and, in the case of the Stem ta Stern, the perfect ghost.

One week after purchasing the property, the owner was awoken with a start by an odd sound she assumed was caused by the wind. She slipped out of bed and went down the stairs to make sure all was well and to get a drink of water. She passed a storage room. She paused. The air drifting under the door was unnaturally cold. And then she heard a sound that chilled her to the bone. *Rat-a-tat-tat, rat-a-tat-tat.* It sounded like someone was tapping on a window, and it appeared to be coming from inside the storage room.

She opened the door and entered the room. What she saw outside the window immediately caught her attention. There was a man hanging by his neck from a large tree, swaying in the wind. She jumped in alarm, but when she looked out the window again, the dead man had disappeared.

It's suspected the man had committed suicide, but no one knows who he was or what exactly happened to him. That doesn't stop the man from frightening guests from time to time. The reports are always the same. Late at night, the bedroom's temperature plummets for no apparent reason. Someone issues a warning on the window:

rat-a-tat-tat, rat-a-tat-tat. But then, instead of hanging from the tree outside, the man suddenly appears in the hall or a room. His face is distorted with pain and his neck is twisted and bruised. It's a terrifying vision that forces guests to scream and shut their eyes tight, and when the guest finally finds the courage to open his or her eyes again, the hanged man is gone.

If the reports from the Stem ta Stern are to be believed, it would appear the prettiest little town in Nova Scotia harbours a secret that's neither pretty nor little.

THE TOMBS OF HELL

Kingston, Ontario

Throughout the year, in fair weather or foul, Kingston tourists are led along shadowy streets and through dark alleys, soaking up every gruesome detail that's shared during one of the country's oldest haunted walks. The tour guides, clad in black robes and carrying a burning lamp, love to chill their groups to the bone with terrifying true stories. But although it's the job of the guides to get under the groups' skin, one ghost is simply too evil, too malicious, to mention.

The ghost is that of George Hewell, a Kingston Penitentiary inmate who was shot to death by the chief keeper in 1897. Hewell was, by all accounts, a particularly bad seed in a jail filled with the worst criminals our country has ever known. He was so bad, in fact, that not even death could stop him from tormenting the guards and his fellow inmates.

Before it closed in 2013, Kingston Pen was the most infamous prison in Canada. It was home to such notorious criminals as Clifford Olson, Paul Bernardo and Russell Williams. Opened in 1835, Kingston Pen predates Confederation and has been designated a national historic site. After 178 years it was deemed to be in a rundown state and too costly to continue operating. The inmates were moved to other jails, but the stories of the terrible things that took place within its imposing limestone walls live on.

In the early days, one form of punishment was to tie a prisoner to a post to be flogged up to forty times with a cat-o'-nine-tails, a nasty whip designed to inflict as much pain and damage on someone's back as possible. Others were disciplined by being branded with a hot iron that burned the flesh, forever marking them as criminals. And there was no shortage of hangings on the premises. Back then an illegal act as mild as stealing a cow or forging a receipt was punishable by death.

Much of this barbaric behaviour was carried out by the first two wardens, father and son Henry and Frank Smith. Henry designed what he called "the box," a wooden coffin that forced inmates to stand upright with no space to move a muscle. Prisoners were left in the box for nearly ten hours and were poked and jabbed by guards through the air holes. Frank allegedly enjoyed shooting at prisoners with a bow and arrow, sticking them with pins and needles as if they were human pincushions and forcibly pouring salt into their mouths.

Although the treatment of prisoners improved over the years, the dark energy created by so much hate and suffering has remained, forever soaked into the stone walls. Some have said entering Kingston Pen is akin to being forced into the tombs of Hell.

Is it the ghost of George Hewell people sense upon walking into the prison? His vengeful spirit has been spotted before. A front page article titled "Did They See a Ghost?" in the *Kingston Daily News* on February 13, 1897, described an eerie encounter with Hewell, who had been dead a year by that time.

With moonlight reflecting brightly off freshly fallen snow, two guards on night duty rounded a corner in the outside courtyard and saw a man in convict's clothing step through the hospital door. The man, described as a "noc-

Kingston Penitentiary

turnal visitor" who had a "strange form," silently crossed the courtyard without paying the guards any attention. They ordered him to identify himself and explain what he was doing out so late, but the man turned and walked back to the hospital door without a word. The guards levelled their rifles to shoot and gave him one last warning. The man turned to face them, touched the hospital door and suddenly disappeared before the guards' disbelieving eyes. They later admitted that they both had immediately recognized the shadowy figure as George Hewell. A late-night search of the prison failed to resolve the mystery.

Before his death, Hewell had been serving a life sentence in Kingston Pen. He had a reputation for attacking anyone within his reach, including guards and fellow inmates. There were at least four recorded incidents in which he tried to kill other convicts, and his murderous instincts could be set off for the most insignificant reasons. He once tried to kill a man for borrowing his library book. He was like a box of dynamite ready to explode at any moment.

The story surrounding Hewell's death is both gruesome and riveting. Early one morning he tried to throw another convict over a three-storey balcony to his death. As punishment he was confined in an isolation cell for some time and then forced to work for the rest of the day in the tailor's shop. This was a mistake, as it gave Hewell, angered and irrational, access to a pair of sharp tailor's shears.

With the shears concealed on his body, Hewell swore and caused a commotion from within his cell through the rest of the evening. After listening to the racket for as long as they could, the guards entered the cell to move Hewell to another location where he could be further punished. Hewell seized his opportunity and attacked the guards with the shears. Fortunately for the guards, he wasn't able to seriously injure anyone before the warden pulled his pistol's trigger and lodged a bullet in Hewell's head.

Normally, a bullet to the head would be enough to kill any man, but Hewell was no regular man. For five full hours Hewell continued to swear and threaten the guards before finally succumbing to the head wound.

With his final breath, Hewell levelled a curse at Kingston Pen. He promised to return from beyond the grave to make everyone pay for killing him — even those who played no part in his death. Dying wouldn't stop him from having his revenge.

Many eerie occurrences since the guards' moonlit patrol have been attributed to the vengeful spirit of Hewell, a man who was never at peace. When he first arrived at Kingston Pen and passed through the front gate of the tombs of Hell, Hewell knew he was serving a life sentence. But he couldn't have known he'd also be serving an after-life sentence.

REBECCA'S CONCRETE GRAVE

Moncton, New Brunswick

There's a slab of concrete on the side of the rarely travelled Gorge Road in northern Moncton. On the surface there's nothing entirely remarkable about the concrete — it appears as if it might have been poured there quite by mistake many years ago and forgotten. A ramshackle fence surrounds the slab, protecting it from farm equipment or snowplows. But the locals know what lies beneath it. Perhaps the only reason the story isn't well known outside New Brunswick is because they'd rather keep the truth as deeply buried as the bones below the concrete at the side of the road.

In 1876, farm girl Rebecca Lutes was sixteen years old. Her family had been lured to southeastern New Brunswick from America with a land grant from the British. There was no shortage of farmable land in Canada, just a shortage of farmers. Many people emigrated from the States, Ireland, Holland, Germany and other far-flung countries to work the land and produce desperately needed crops. Many of the immigrants brought their superstitious beliefs with them to Canada. Misfortune, bad weather, illness — these could all be attributed to evil forces.

The summer of 1876 had been especially dry, providing little food in the fields and leaving Moncton susceptible to flash fires. A few families lost their barns and homes to raging forest fires, which only made the food shortage worse. As fall turned to winter, a new problem arose: farmers throughout the area were waking in the morning to find that their livestock had disappeared overnight. The community was desperate to find something — or rather, someone — to blame.

Compounding the situation were reports of bizarre lights floating along the roads after dusk and rumours of demonic rituals being practised deep in the woods. The townsfolk, at their wits' end, agreed that there must be a witch among them.

The story isn't clear on how they came to believe Rebecca was the guilty party, but it was said that she had been seen practising witchcraft and had stolen the animals herself, using their blood for sacrificial purposes in her dark ceremonies. She was tried, found guilty and sentenced to death.

One heartbreaking version of the tale claims that Rebecca was hanged from a tree on her own property as her family was forced to watch. Her body was then cut down and buried at the base of the tree. But the townsfolk feared a dead witch almost as much as a live one, so they took extreme precautions with the burial.

First, her body wasn't placed face up as is customary, but face down. This was to prevent the witch from digging her way back up to the surface should she return from the dead. Instead she'd dig her way straight down to Hell. Second, they poured a four-block concrete casing into the hole to further prevent her from rising from her grave.

Despite their best efforts to seal her six feet under for eternity, the locals began seeing Rebecca wandering the fields at night, and these reports continue today. Sometimes Rebecca takes the form of a thick, misty cloud, and other times people see floating orbs of light that are attributed to her. The land around her concrete grave is often unnaturally cold. People have seen their breath on muggy summer days and car windows have frozen over as vehicles pass her resting spot. Fresh bloodstains often appear on the surface of the concrete grave only to fade away moments later. There's an old abandoned church across the street, and Rebecca has been spotted peering down at the living from an upper window. But she hasn't always been spotted alone; many have seen a black cat sitting on the concrete, both during the day and at night. When approached, the cat suddenly disappears. Some people believe the phantom feline is waiting for the day when Rebecca returns to this plain permanently.

The concrete grave remains on the side of Gorge Road to this day. Visiting it after midnight has become a rite of passage for local teenagers. It's a story so spine-chillingly compelling that it can't remain a secret from the rest of the country for long.

THE FAMILY THAT HAUNTS TOGETHER

Colwood, British Columbia

For most young cadets training for a life in the military, the people they fear the most are their superiors. This wasn't the case at Hatley Castle, a mansion located on the grounds of what was once Royal Roads Military College, a naval training facility from the 1940s to 1995.

Who could be more frightening than a drill sergeant barking orders and demanding push-ups? The family who built and lived in Hatley Castle, that's who. The family who died many years before the military college opened. The family reunited in the afterlife and none too pleased with the new tenants of their beautiful home.

James Dunsmuir was at one time the most influential and wealthy man in the entire province of British Columbia. He was born while his father (who would become a Vancouver Island coal baron) and mother emigrated from Scotland to B.C. in 1851. He stepped out of his father's shadow to become a powerful industrialist and politician, holding the positions of both Premier and Lieutenant-Governor of British Columbia in close succession. The mansion Dunsmuir built in 1908 for his large family, Hatley Castle, was designed in the Scottish baronial style, reflecting his heritage.

"Money doesn't matter. Just build what I want," he reportedly told the contractors. Dunsmuir, his wife, Laura, and their children (they had twelve, nine of whom survived infancy) loved their home. It's not hard to understand why.

The mansion boasted fifty rooms on 640 acres that also had farms, a modern dairy and its own slaughterhouse. A fishing lodge was built on property along the Cowichan River. The gardens were so extensive and magnificent that Dunsmuir had to employ one hundred gardeners and groundskeepers. It was the type of home that would be hard to leave behind. For the Dunsmuirs, the act of packing up and moving on would prove impossible, even in death.

Despite the luxury in which he lived, James Dunsmuir's final days were not happy. One of his two sons had died in 1915 when the RMS *Lusitania* sank and the other, an alcoholic, had left home to roam the world aimlessly, tarnishing the family's name. And Dunsmuir's daughters had married and moved far away, leading lives that Dunsmuir believed to be frivolous. He died in his fishing lodge in 1920. At the time of his death, he was still the richest man in the province, but in a few short years his entire fortune had been squandered by his children. Hatley Castle was sold to the government in 1940. The years between Dunsmuir's death and the selling of Hatley Castle were harder on no one more than Dunsmuir's widow, Laura. She had become accustomed to the elegant life she had enjoyed, entertaining celebrities and the British aristocracy in her home. She fell into depression, grew very ill and passed away in 1937.

Soon after her death, a maid reported feeling terribly uncomfortable while working alone in the house. She couldn't shake the feeling that someone was watching her as she worked, and there were some rooms that she couldn't bring herself to enter.

When Hatley Castle became Royal Roads Military College in 1941, the tales of peculiar incidents began to increase. Cadets were often overcome by a discomforting sensation in the middle of the night, as if they had suddenly stepped into an ice-cold spider web. And imagine waking to see an old woman staring down at you before vanishing into the night? Many cadets have experienced just that, and their descriptions of the old ghost perfectly match Laura Dunsmuir. They say she didn't look happy to see so many young men living in her house. One night, she decided to take matters into her own hands.

A cadet who was acting as senior duty officer fell asleep but was awoken suddenly a few hours later when someone pulled his leg. He sat bolt upright and blinked in the darkness, expecting the culprit to be one of his superiors or a fellow cadet, but he couldn't believe his eyes: it was the ghost of Mrs. Dunsmuir, hell-bent on dragging him out of his bed and out of her house. He tried to free his leg but, despite his strength and Mrs. Dunsmuir's small stature, the spectre held onto him with an unearthly ferocity. Finally the young cadet was able to shake himself free from her cold, dead hands, and Laura Dunsmuir dissipated in the air before him. When the cadet shared his experience the next morning, he discovered he wasn't alone — many other cadets had also been attacked and pulled from their beds by the deceased widow.

Although Mrs. Dunsmuir is the angriest ghost that haunts Hatley Castle, she's not alone. James Dunsmuir has been seen floating through the basement walls, surrounded by bright white light, and some of their children have also been spotted. The property has now become a university, and the students enrolled there often report ghostly run-ins with the Dunsmuirs. The family that

Hatley Castle

haunts together, sticks together, even beyond the grave. The students and professors can only hope that James Dunsmuir and his children don't become as violent as Laura Dunsmuir has proven herself to be.

HOSPITAL OF THE DEAD

Inglewood, Alberta

A bloody handprint smeared on a door, dried-up blood caked on every surface in a room and bugs crawling everywhere. These are the horrific sights that confronted an anonymous young thrill-seeker who snuck into the Charles Camsell Hospital in Inglewood late one night with her older brother and his friends. The flashlights gripped in their trembling hands did little to brighten the ghostly atmosphere of the abandoned hospital. After describing the bloody scene above, the girl could say no more, simply concluding that there are things in the creepy building that you don't want to see. She still has nightmares about it.

She isn't the only one to warn against venturing into the abandoned hospital. Others have reported that the floors and walls on the second floor, which used to be the hospital's surgical ward, are covered in old bloodstains. Take a trip up to the fourth floor and you're now standing in what used to be the hospital's psych ward. Stay a while and chances are good you'll hear soft screams slowly getting louder and closer. If you somehow manage to stand your ground, a teenage girl who was once a patient will slowly creep out of the shadows. Look closely at her hands and you'll see why she's still screaming years after her death: before she died many years ago, she ripped each of her own fingernails free from her fingertips.

Confronted by such a ghastly image, it's safe to say no one would be able to resist the urge to flee, but it's best to take the stairs (even though barbed wire has been wrapped around the handrails in an attempt to keep people out). The elevators to the morgue occasionally travel up and down on their own, as if the spirits of all the bodies once kept there can't stay put in the basement.

What makes Charles Camsell Hospital such a magnet for paranormal activity? Although it was a place that helped many people get better over the years, there are also a few dark and troubling secrets etched into its history.

Between the years of 1945 and 1967 it was an experimental hospital offering an occupational therapy program for Aboriginal patients. Shock treatment was administered without consent and there were isolation rooms where terrified patients were locked in the dark on their own. It is widely suspected that the staff not only abused the Aboriginal population, but also murdered some of the patients. If that's not upsetting enough, it's also rumoured that there's an unmarked mass grave of Aboriginal children near what used to be the staff garden.

It's no surprise that stories of vengeful spirits at the Charles Camsell Hospital continue to surface. Most recently, a man who was contracted to clean part of the building one night with a few co-workers shared his story. The phones, left behind and not used in more than twenty years, rang repeatedly while they worked through the night. When the cleaners picked up the ringing phones, there was no dial tone — the lines were dead. In one of the rooms, the cleaners saw the outline of a small child suddenly form on a dust-covered chair. When they entered the basement — the old morgue — they all had trouble breathing, and a deep, bloody cut suddenly appeared on the back of a woman's hand.

Charles Camsell Hospital

That was enough to send them running from the building. They jumped in their vehicle and sped away, leaving the Charles Camsell Hospital looming on the horizon behind them.

But for as long as the hospital could be seen in their rear-view mirror, the team leader's cell phone rang and rang and rang. When he finally mustered the courage to look at his phone's screen, it read:

1 missed call: The Charles Camsell Hospital

DUEL TO THE DEATH

St. John's, Newfoundland and Labrador

There was a time, not too long ago, that the honourable way for two gentlemen to settle a serious dispute was to stand back to back, walk ten paces, turn . . . and fire pistols at each other. Instead of firearms, others preferred to brandish steel. Regardless of the method, these so called "honourable" duels often ended in bloodshed, death and sometimes, historic hauntings.

The last duel to be held on Canadian soil took place in St. John's in 1873, but it wasn't fatal for either duellist. Another St. John's duel in 1826, however, did end in death — a death so unnecessary and tragic that the loser couldn't bring himself to leave this plain.

Sipping rum toddies and huddled around a blazing fireplace during a bitter Newfoundland night, the officers of the British army and Royal Veteran Company stationed at Fort Townshend passed their time by gambling at cards. Among those present were Captain Mark Rudkin and Ensign John Philpot, and as cold as it was outside, the tension between these two was heated. Not only were they adversaries in the card game of lansquenet being played, but they were also competing for the affections of the Irish daughter of a St. John's businessman who lived in Quidi Vidi Village. This rivalry had already caused Philpot, the younger of the two men, to insult Rudkin at a public event, an occurrence for which he had later begrudgingly apologized. On the night of the card game, there was certainly no love lost between the two military men, and the presence of alcohol and gambling did nothing to decrease their contempt for one another.

Philpot was on a losing streak, while fortune smiled upon Rudkin. The other men in the game folded their hands and gradually bowed out until only Philpot, still losing, and Rudkin, still winning, remained. Philpot was desperate to end on a winning note to recoup some of his losses, and the pot had grown to nearly three pounds, quite a large sum in those days. Rudkin dealt the final hand, and his own happened to be the winning one.

It couldn't be so. Philpot was sure of it. Rudkin, out of his dislike for Philpot, must have cheated. Philpot accused Rudkin of rigging the final hand and tried to grab the money. Rudkin scoffed, denied the charge, and made for the door with his winnings. Enraged, drunk and blinded by his hatred for Rudkin, Philpot threw a glass of water in his face.

Rudkin, to his credit, kept his cool and tried to diffuse the situation, but Philpot wouldn't let it go and continued to goad the captain. With the other officers playing witness and his honour and reputation at stake, Rudkin challenged Philpot to a duel. Philpot agreed without reservation.

Early the next morning, March 30, the two men met a mile outside of town near Brine's Tavern at Robinson's Hill. Rudkin had once again cooled down and offered to call off the duel. Philpot, however, was still fuming and insisted that Rudkin must have cheated. He refused the captain's offer.

With loaded pistols, they stood back to back, walked apart ten paces and turned. Philpot fired first. Luckily for Rudkin the shot just grazed his collar. Now, with time on his side and the perfect opportunity to shoot Philpot, Rudkin took the higher road. He raised his pistol above his head and fired his shot into the air. The duel had ended without bloodshed.

Anyone else in Philpot's position would consider himself fortunate to still be breathing, but Philpot saw it as a second opportunity to rid the world of Rudkin. He insisted that a second round take place despite the fact that such an act wasn't customary. (Traditionally, if the opponents of a duel survived the first round, both would retain their honour and the dispute was considered to be resolved.) With no other option, Rudkin had to accept the challenge. But this time he did not purposely fire his shot wide. His bullet found a home in Philpot's chest, buried deep in his right lung. The ensign flew backwards and died not long after he hit the ground, a victim of his own stupidity and stubbornness. He was buried, coincidentally, on April Fool's Day.

Rudkin was charged with murder and a short trial followed. Public sympathy was initially on Philpot's side, but it quickly shifted to Rudkin's as the full story — with Rudkin's many attempts to save the young ensign — came to light. On April 17, Rudkin was carried from the courthouse on the shoulders of his friends and supporters after being found not guilty, but disturbing reports began to surface from Robinson's Hill, the location of the duel.

Rudkin's horse had become skittish as he rode to the duel on that chilly March morning, as if the animal could sense the tragedy that lay ahead. Others have reported the same odd behaviour from their horses near the spot where Philpot's blood soaked the ground. Some have come face to face with Philpot's ghost and noticed a bloody hole on the chest of his military uniform. It's been said that he wanders the streets at night near the place where he died, still angry and eternally longing for a rematch. After all, he was not only "cheated" in his pursuit of love, the card game and the duel, but when Rudkin was found to be innocent of murder, Philpot was cheated out of his posthumous justice as well. Some grudges carry on beyond the grave.

THE MOB PRINCESS

Fort Saskatchewan, Alberta

Many male convicts were hanged years ago at the North West Mounted Police outpost in Fort Saskatchewan, but only one woman. In 1923 Florence Lassandro, a woman dubbed the "Mob Princess," was executed for a crime she may or may not have committed. She was only twenty-two years old.

In fact Florence was the only woman ever to be hanged in the province of Alberta. She was born Florence Costanzo in Italy and moved to the Canadian province with her family when she was a young girl. At fifteen years of age, she was still a young girl when she married Charles Lassandro.

Charles worked for a businessman named Emilio Picariello who, among other things, owned an ice cream company and the Alberta Hotel. But his legitimate businesses were merely a front for a successful bootlegging operation he had started. Emilio made a lot of money sneaking booze from Alberta, where it could be purchased legally, into the state of Montana during the early part of the nineteenth century.

Charles introduced his wife to the mob boss Emilio, which set her down a dark path. Florence earned the name Mob Princess by working her way up within Emilio's criminal organization and performing smuggling runs herself. It's possible Florence, who never seemed too fond of her husband, was actually in love with Emilio's son, Steve, who was also a player in his father's bootlegging business.

In 1921 Steve Picariello was shot by Alberta Provincial Police Constable Steve Lawson during a high-speed chase. Wounded, Steve Picariello managed to escape to British Columbia. Upon hearing that his son had been shot, and believing him dead, Emilio teamed up with Florence and tracked down Constable Lawson. They confronted him in front of his house. An argument broke out and Lawson was fatally shot in the back. The horrific scene played out before the mortified eyes of Lawson's nine-year-old daughter, Pearl.

Emilio and Florence were both convicted of the murder, although Florence proclaimed until her last day that she was innocent and that it was Emilio who had shot Constable Lawson. Despite the fact that there was no conclusive proof of who shot the constable, the jury found both Emilio and Florence guilty of the crime. The Mob Princess was hanged on May 2, 1923, at the Fort Saskatchewan jail before a small group of witnesses hand-picked by the hangman.

But did she truly leave her life behind, or was hers a story steeped too heavily in crime, bloodshed and unrequited love to ever leave this world?

The Fort Saskatchewan Museum & Historic Site now sits on the land where Florence was hanged. It's a picturesque historic village with eight heritage buildings (including the warden's house and a portion of the jail) decorated with period furniture. Visitors walking the grounds get a sense of what life was like in the bygone era, and schoolchildren enjoy field trips to the Museum & Historic Site throughout the year. But if you stay past sundown, you might experience a "bygone" event you wish you could forget.

There have been many reports of lights turning on and off, objects moving on their own and faces seen in windows. A clairvoyant and medium visited the grounds and picked up on many unexplained cold spots, thick atmospheres and spiritual energy in the buildings. One woman who used to work at the museum suddenly quit because of the ghost haunting the area.

Even Curator Kris Nygren, who calls herself a skeptic, has to admit that those who have seen eerie things on the property are "believable" people and reliable sources. And Darlene Briere is perhaps the most believable and reliable of all. Darlene conducts research for the museum and volunteers for special events and programs. One Halloween Darlene was involved with Fright Night, a special children's sleepover on the grounds. While taking a late-night walk

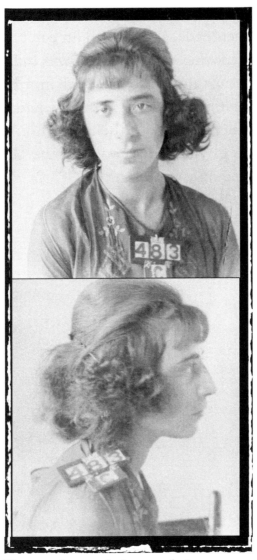

Florence Lessandro's mug shots

between the blacksmith's shop and the jail, she saw an odd mist take shape in the moonlit woods and snapped a couple of pictures. When Darlene examined one of the photos, she saw the clear image of a young woman's face within the fog. It was, she strongly believes, the face of Florence.

Later that night, while making sure all the young guests were safe in their beds, she entered an empty building and saw a curtain moving, as if a person was hiding behind it. Suddenly, the curtain fell to the floor in a heap. Darlene lifted the curtain with trembling fingers and there, for the briefest of moments, she saw the face again.

If you dare to visit the location of the Mob Princess's execution, so could you.

THE MAN IN GREY

Saskatoon, Saskatchewan

Upon entering the Delta Bessborough Hotel in downtown Saskatoon, you might want to keep your eyes on your feet. There's a large crack in the marble floor of the main lobby. You wouldn't want to trip on the spot where a man fell to his death many years ago.

The Bessborough — or "Bess" as it's affectionately called — was completed in 1932 but didn't open to the public for three years due to the economic hardships of the Great Depression. Designed to resemble a Bavarian fortress, it's well known for its imposing facade and castle-like appearance. It's also well known for the crack in the floor and the ghost of the man who might have created it with his head.

There's no shortage of people who have seen an elderly

gentleman walking through the banquet level late at night. The reports are always the same: he's tall, slender and well dressed in a grey suit and fedora, a popular fashion during the 1930s. "The Man in Grey," as he's called, is always pleasant, smiles at passersby and will occasionally offer a quiet hello, but is otherwise silent. When guests mention the oddly attired but nice old man they passed in the hall, employees of the Bess chuckle and inform the guests that they've just been greeted by a ghost.

That's perhaps the most striking thing about The Man in Grey. Guests and employees alike are amazed by how lifelike he appears, unlike other ghosts who are transparent or bear the injuries that claimed their lives.

One question lingers in the air like smoke from a snuffed candle: Did The Man in Grey crack the marble floor? Bess employees seem to think so. They share a story about an employee — a nice old man from the 1930s who dressed impeccably — who was sent upstairs late one night to deal with noise complaints. There was a party in one of the rooms that was disturbing the other guests on the same floor. The employee knocked on the door and kindly asked if the revellers could keep the noise down. The men answered his request with an insane action rather than words. Two men picked up the employee and threw him over the balcony. He fell seven storeys to his death, cracking his skull and the floor below. Current-day Bess employees think the ghost belongs to this kind and unfortunate man who was simply doing his job.

Colin Tranborg, founder of Paranormal Saskatchewan, saw The Man in Grey late one evening and has also heard

The Delta Bessborough Hotel

a compelling first-hand account from a group of ghost hunters. They snuck into a storage closet on the hotel's top floor and saw a man staring at them from outside through a window. Terrified, they wondered how he wasn't falling to his death — there was simply no way to explain it. Unless he'd *already* fallen to his death back in the 1930s.

There are other ghosts staying at the Bess. Guests have reported running into a disturbed woman in one of the upper floors' hallways. She screams bloody murder when approached and then suddenly disappears. And the spirits of two small children are thought to live in one of the stairwells, playing together for all eternity.

But there's no doubt The Man in Grey is the Bess's most famous ghost, perhaps because he's such a happy soul. People seem more inclined to speak about him than the other spirits. After all, if you came face to face with a ghost in the dead of night, wouldn't you rather be greeted with a "hello" than a ghastly shriek?

THE SHOW MUST GO ON AND ON AND ON

Dawson City, Yukon

The Yukon Territory is a mysterious and wild land. During the weeks before and after the winter solstice, the capital city, Whitehorse, has only five and a half hours of sunlight per day. It's the promised land for things that go bump in the night, giving ghosts with an aversion to daylight free reign to roam the pitch-black streets for more than eighteen hours a day. And the Klondike Gold Rush of the late nineteenth century left a string of abandoned outposts — many still perfectly preserved today — that are ghost towns in more than name alone.

Dawson City, with a population of about one thousand, is far from a ghost town, but it's also a far cry from the forty thousand people who lived there in 1898. The gold rush kicked off in 1896 when three men found gold in

Bonanza Creek. Within two years Dawson City was filled with miners looking to stake their claim and entrepreneurs hoping to cash in on the population boom. But the Yukon was a dangerous land, and mining was dangerous work. Many people lost their lives during the gold rush, often in brutal fashion, and it was common to bury the corpses in unmarked graves. It's believed that an undercurrent of supernatural energy hums through the city's bones to this day on account of the bloodshed and tragedies that occurred during the gold rush, and one ghost takes centre stage in Dawson City. It's a ghost that appears to be aflame. A ghost of one of the city's most famous previous residents.

But the ghost doesn't belong to popular writers Pierre Berton or Jack London, both of whom once called Dawson City home. Nor is it the ghost of any of the Dawson City Nuggets, a hockey team that travelled to our nation's capital in 1905 by ship, train and dogsled to lose the most lopsided series in Stanley Cup history to the Ottawa Silver Seven. The flaming ghost is that of Kathleen Rockwell, better known as Klondike Kate.

As a young girl, Kate was a free spirit and a tomboy, more comfortable playing with boys than girls and frustrated by the lack of opportunities for women in the late 1800s. Her temper was as fiery as her bright red hair, and her rebellious nature kept her from settling in one spot for long. She was expelled from school before trying, unsuccessfully, to break into show business in New York City. In 1899, hearing of the gold rush and envisioning the influx of miners to Dawson City desperate for entertainment, she travelled to the Yukon. However, Kate was refused entry by the Royal Canadian Mounted Police, who were trying to control the number of people rushing into the territory.

Never one to be intimidated by authority nor hindered by rules, Kate is reputed to have disguised herself as a boy and hidden upon a boat that had gained clearance to travel from Alaska to the Yukon.

Not long after arriving in Dawson City, Kate joined the Savoy Theatrical Company and began performing in daily shows at the Palace Grand Theatre. Her notoriety and fame sparked as quickly as a match, thanks in large part to her signature "flame dance." She spun many yards of red chiffon around her body to create the illusion that she was on fire in the middle of the stage, and it wasn't long before everyone knew Klondike Kate. Other nicknames followed, such as the Darling of Dawson. And, thanks in no small part to her, Dawson City became known as the Paris of the North.

Dawson City's new reputation for being an entertainment centre was also created by the work of struggling bartender Alexander Pantages, who became a theatre owner and eventually a movie mogul. Kate and Pantages grew very close and it seemed like her star would never fall nor lose its shine, but their relationship was as turbulent as a Yukon winter storm. Pantages left Kate at the same time the gold rush came to a screeching halt.

After a few years of mining, it had become apparent that there wasn't as much gold in the area as everyone had hoped. Dawson City saw its population plummet as quickly as it had risen. The forty thousand people who lived there in 1898 all but disappeared overnight, leaving only eight thousand residents by 1899 and 615 by 1911. Dawson City was no longer a city, and although the Palace Grand Theatre remained, Klondike Kate was left without an audience. She eventually packed up and left town. After another string of unsuccessful attempts to find her footing in show business, she ended her days playing the part of a social outcast and recluse. She died on February 21, 1957.

But the show must go on. Although she died in America, it's said that Kate's spirit returned to the beloved location of her glory days, the Palace Grand Theatre in Dawson City. Her ghost is believed to haunt her old dressing room and people have reported seeing a blazing red swirl in the middle of the stage during the night when no one else is in the theatre. Bronwyn Jones was a stage manager of the Palace Grand from 2002 to 2004, and she believes the intensely short time frame of the Klondike Gold Rush — and the amount of history that happened in such a short span — might be part of the reason for the spiritual energy that's still felt in the building's walls.

Dawson City is now a major tourist attraction, drawing sixty thousand visitors each year. The Palace Grand Theatre still puts on performances, many of which reflect life in the Old West. And then, once everyone has left after the final show of the evening, Klondike Kate takes the stage and performs her fire dance for an audience of none.

Klondike Kate

THE SHADOW IN YOUR BEDROOM

Iqaluit, Nunavut

With extremely bitter winters and very short summers, the city of Iqaluit, capital of Nunavut, is too cold to grow trees. Amongst the snow, ice and rock you'll only find hardened, scraggly bushes. Winter temperatures average -30°C to -45°C. The howling Arctic winds chill to the bone and exposed skin can freeze in minutes, but a shadowy man who watches people while they sleep has been even more effective at turning people's blood to ice.

There used to be a townhouse complex in Iqaluit called White Row that many former tenants believed to be haunted. The entire complex tragically burned to the ground in 2012 in a blaze that the city's fire chief deemed to be suspicious.

Bumps in the night, knocking on the walls and phantom footsteps in the halls were common bedtime sounds in White Row. Most people brushed the odd noises off as the sounds of an old building or rationalized that they must've been caused by the winter wind, but others saw what — or rather, *who* — was the source of the disturbances within White Row.

There was a man, a shadowy man — a shadowy man who watched people at night. Most often it was young children and teenagers who saw the shadowy man. Imagine: one moment you're alone, the next moment you see the shadowy man in your doorway, and the moment after that he's gone. He never made a sound or moved a muscle, and he seemed incapable of passing through doors or entering rooms. It appeared as if his sole purpose was to stare at the living after they'd gone to bed.

One young girl reported seeing the shadowy man for the first time shortly after her family moved into White Row. He appeared in her doorway while she was alone and freaked her out so much that she ran straight to her sister's room. One night, as the girl was talking to her cousin, she spotted the shadowy man in her closet out of the corner of her eye, staring out from the darkness within. He appeared in her room every single night until the family moved into a new home.

Despite her initial fear, the girl said she grew accustomed to the shadowy man and learned to live with the unexplained phenomena. He didn't give off an evil energy, she said, although his appearances were often preceded by an unusual feeling. The girl even began to believe that the shadowy man was there to protect her.

Everyone who saw the shadowy man described him as tall and pale, but his most disconcerting characteristic was his neck. A deep purple bruise ringed it, as did the deep outline of a rope. It was believed he used to live in White Row and committed suicide somewhere in the building, trapping his soul within. Whether he was unable to pass through doorways or voluntarily chose not to (and even if he was there to protect the people he watched), his presence certainly didn't make it easy to fall asleep at night.

A shadow passing by a bedroom door or the sound of something stirring in the darkness of a closet might simply be products of imagination . . . but then again, it might be something else, something unexplainable.

Something real.

HAUNTED NIGHTMARES

Selkirk, Manitoba

Like many infamously haunted locations, St. Andrew's on the Red attracts a regular procession of ghost hunters. People have seen chilling sights and heard unnatural sounds, but most distressingly, many have suffered from a recurring nightmare that keeps them up all night for weeks following their visit. A nightmare of an unseen presence rattling the cemetery gates so viciously that it threatens to tear them off their hinges.

Built between 1845 and 1849, St. Andrew's on the Red in Selkirk (twenty-two kilometres northeast of Winnipeg) is the oldest stone church in Western Canada. Its small cemetery is filled with locals that succumbed to plagues such as influenza, diphtheria, typhoid and tuberculosis, as well as many notable people who played a role in Manitoba's history. It's little wonder that it's also a hot spot for paranormal sightings.

When the Hudson's Bay Company and the North West Company amalgamated in the 1820s, many workers either retired or lost their jobs. Some of these people settled with their families in what is now Selkirk along the Red River. Archdeacon William Cockran built a wooden church in 1831, the outline of which can still be found directly behind the present stone church. When you set foot inside this holy place, you're immediately struck by the history within, as much of the interior has remained unchanged since 1849.

Old, gnarled trees cast shadows on the cemetery grounds. You'll find the crumbling tombstones of Archdeacon Cockran; E.H.G.G. Hay, first leader of Manitoba's Official Opposition Party in 1870; Alexander Christie, Chief Factor of the Hudson's Bay Company; and Captain William Kennedy, an Arctic explorer who searched for Sir John Franklin's lost expedition in 1851. Stick around after nightfall and this quiet, peaceful burial place becomes decidedly less so.

There are spine-tingling reports from late-night churchgoers who have seen a man in black and a woman in white drifting a foot above the cemetery's ground. Rumour has it that the woman died during the church's construction and sometimes appears on the balcony during services. Others have seen a ghost car appear out of thin air and pull up to the cemetery's gate. It sits and idles for a moment — perhaps looking to pick someone up or to drop someone (recently deceased, most likely) off — before disappearing.

St. Andrew's on the Red

The strangest regular sighting in the St. Andrew's on the Red cemetery is a pair of red eyes peering out from behind tombstones and trees, silently watching those who walk the grounds at night.

While enrolled in the Creative Communications program at Red River College, Jenn Twardowski and a classmate filmed the cemetery for a school project. Even under the safety and comfort of daylight they had a disconcerting experience. They were followed by a weird, unexplainable noise similar to a hammer striking a nail in a coffin. Both of the students were simultaneously relieved and creeped out when they learned the other had heard the spooky sound as well.

Although Jenn set out to capture one of the spirits on film, she should count her blessings that she did not. Those who have seen the man in black, the woman in white, the phantom car or the red eyes have all suffered from hideous nightmares. These night terrors are filled with the violent rattling of the church's gates. Some believe the nightmares are a plea for help from the church's ghosts. Others see them as a dark omen and a dire warning never to return.

DEAD-EYED DOLLS

Ottawa, Ontario

The Bytown Museum couldn't have a more picturesque location in our nation's capital. Housed in the oldest stone building in Ottawa, the museum is on the lower locks of the Rideau Canal at the Ottawa River, nestled in the heart of downtown between Parliament Hill and the Chateau Laurier Hotel.

But the petite museum's beauty and charm are in direct contrast with the truly terrifying experiences that visitors and employees have reported. In fact, it's considered by many paranormal experts to be the most haunted location in the entire country. Something lives in the museum's displays, skulking through the artifacts and taking possession of the antique dolls that sit in silent rows, watching everyone who wanders up to the second floor unawares.

The building was constructed in 1827 by the British military as a supply storehouse and treasury during the construction of the Rideau Canal. Death was always hanging over the building in those early years, as nearly one thousand workers died in gruesome construction accidents and from diseases such as malaria. Undeterred by the tragic deaths of so many workers, the military continued work on the canal under the leadership of Lieutenant Colonel John By in order to defend against invasion from the United States. Although Lt. Col. By died in 1836, some believe his ghost still lingers by the still waters of the Rideau Canal.

Today the Bytown Museum houses a permanent collection of artifacts celebrating Ottawa's history, and it's not uncommon for visitors to be overcome by an uneasy feeling while they're observing the displays. On the second floor is a collection of antique dolls that has caused some of the greatest unease. If it's very quiet and you're all alone, close your eyes and strain your ears. You might hear the faint sounds of a child crying. Open your eyes and you might even catch one of the dolls winking at you as if you're in on some ghastly joke. Those who have heard the crying and seen the blinking eyes believe the spooky porcelain dolls are possessed by the spirits of dead children.

Other visitors have said they have been pushed, grabbed or tripped from behind when alone, typically in the creepy old money vault and the stairwell. Some museum-goers have heard an angry, bodiless voice shout, "Get out! Get out!" But the majority of the paranormal reports come from the museum staff, and the most hair-raising activity tends to occur after the public has left for the night.

One employee noticed a man sitting in the library after she had closed up. She asked him to leave, and he obliged without a word, silently walking to the door. A second after he stepped outside, she realized she hadn't seen the man enter the museum while they were open — an impossibility in such a small, intimate building — so she flung the door open to ask how he had gotten in. Although it had only been a brief moment since the man had left and she could see a far distance in every direction, the man had completely vanished.

Glen Shackleton, chairman of the board of directors, has no doubt the Bytown Museum is haunted, and he has a couple of chilling stories to back up this claim. One night he and three others were the only four people in the building. They closed a sliding door and it immediately began to vibrate violently as if someone on the other side was hitting it. A review of the security camera footage showed that no one was there, but as soon as the assault on the door ended they heard heavy footsteps walking away. The late-night encounter with an unseen presence was enough to send Glen's three companions running from the museum.

Glen believes, as many others do, that the ghost who causes these disturbances is Duncan McNab. Duncan was a supply manager during the construction of the Rideau Canal. But Glen also thinks there might be at least one other prominent ghost within the walls of the museum, someone who had a much larger role in the canal's construction.

Another night he was having a casual chat with a

museum employee about the ghost of McNab when the woman's computer inexplicably turned off. A moment later it turned itself back on, but her normal desktop didn't appear. Instead, the monitor was blank other than the words "Lt. Col. John By" repeated over and over on the screen. It was as if the colonel himself was listening in on the conversation and wanted to make it clear that McNab's ghost isn't the only spirit haunting the Bytown Museum. Nor does it seem that either man is ready to leave his life's work behind.

THE BLOODY BATTLEFIELD

Quebec City, Quebec

Although it only lasted a mere fifteen minutes, the Battle of the Plains of Abraham was one of the bloodiest in Canada's history. It's said the lawns grow so lush and green today thanks to the litres of French and British blood that were spilled there on September 13, 1759. It's estimated that more than 1 300 soldiers were killed or injured during the battle. That's roughly three people every two seconds. With so much life lost in such a violent way and in such a short period of time, it's little wonder Battlefields Park, named in commemoration of the historic battle, is widely considered to be the most haunted location in Quebec.

The Battle of the Plains of Abraham was fought on a plateau just outside the walls of Quebec City on land that was owned by a farmer named Abraham (which explains the battle's name). Although it was over quickly, it was the culmination of a three-month siege by the British and was a pivotal moment in Canadian history. It's interesting to ponder how Canada, known as New France at the time, would be different today if the British had lost the battle and hadn't taken control of Quebec from the French.

That's not to say that the British didn't suffer during the battle. Far from it. The two sides had nearly an identical number of casualties and wounded soldiers, and both leaders, British General James Wolfe and French Lieutenant General Louis-Joseph de Montcalm, died from wounds suffered on the battlefield. Moreover, they both welcomed death as if the Grim Reaper were an old friend.

Wolfe was struck in the stomach and chest by two shots near the beginning of the battle and fell to the ground. Upon hearing a soldier shout, "They run, see how they run," Wolfe opened his eyes and asked who was running. When he heard the French lines had broken and they were fleeing, he sighed in relief and said, "Now, God be praised, I will die in peace." These were his final words. He died immediately after uttering them.

During the retreat, Montcalm was struck repeatedly in his lower abdomen and thigh. He managed to escape but died from the wounds early the next morning. When he was informed by the surgeons trying to save his life that his wounds were mortal, he calmly replied, "I am glad of it." The surgeons added that he didn't have long to live. "So much the better," Montcalm said gravely. "I am happy that I shall not live to see the surrender of Quebec." His body was buried in a crater created by an

General James Wolfe

*Lieutenant General
Louis-Joseph de
Montcalm*

exploded bombshell, a grim location of his own choosing.

Battlefields Park's concealed location and many hidden nooks and crannies have made it notorious for illicit activities such as duels, muggings and even executions. These dastardly doings have given the park a dark reputation. It's believed that the most dangerous time to visit is September — not because of an increase in criminal activity, but an increase in *paranormal* activity.

On cold nights in September, especially near the thirteenth and the anniversary of the battle that took place in 1759, the spirits of the fallen soldiers rise from the once blood-soaked ground to re-enact the warfare. People have smelled sulfur hanging heavily in the air and have heard cannons firing. Pallid-looking ghosts in eighteenth-century uniforms have been seen wandering the plain and rushing to and from the entrances to the tunnels beneath the park.

Is it possible that General Wolfe and Lieutenant General Montcalm, two men who weren't afraid of death, rise from their graves to lead their spectral armies into battle on the anniversary of their battle? Go for a daytime stroll through Battlefields Park and take a good look at the grass beneath your feet. It is unnaturally green, particularly after September 13. Could it be that it's not mere fertilizer that makes each blade so vivid and bright?

GHOST TOWN TUNNELS

Tranquille, British Columbia

Fifteen minutes west of downtown Kamloops, British Columbia, in a scenic valley surrounded by water and trees and mountains, is a ghost town known as Tranquille. More than forty buildings have sat idle for years. Long ago they fell into disrepair and their boarded up doors and shattered windows have given the town a creepy, unwelcoming face. Even under the comfort of the midday sun, it's easy to picture the many ghosts that have been seen here over the years. But if you enter one of the abandoned Tranquille buildings, the ghosts who dwell within might not be behind your back but *below your feet.*

The town notorious for hauntings gets its ironic name from the Tranquille River, which flows into Kamloops Lake. In 1907 the Tranquille Sanatorium was built to treat people diagnosed with tuberculosis (or TB). TB was a widespread epidemic in the early 1900s and the sanatorium filled with patients so quickly that an entire town blossomed around it. There were homes, dormitories, a schoolhouse, a cafeteria, a gymnasium, a fire hall, a large laundromat, a cemetery . . . even farms and their own steam plant, making the town completely self-sustained. This was designed to minimize the town's need to be in contact with the outside world. Simply put, people came to Tranquille to die.

According to official records, nearly 1,600 people, mostly children, died of TB in Tranquille. In order to move the bodies between buildings without creating a commotion or disturbing the other patients, nearly two kilometres of tunnels were built beneath Tranquille's streets. While townsfolk went about their business above ground, the dearly departed went about theirs below ground.

After the Tranquille Sanatorium closed in the 1950s, the property changed hands a few times (becoming a hospital to treat the mentally ill, and an ill-fated amusement park, of all things). In 1983 the property was completely abandoned and the buildings began to fall into disrepair. Tranquille became a desolate place, haunted by the tragic memories of what had transpired there, and this, of course, attracted a new interest in the area. Curiosity seekers, ghost hunters and teens looking for a place to spook each other snuck into the town after nightfall. Many were too afraid of the unsettling vibe in the air to ever leave their cars, but those who were brave enough were treated to a truly eerie experience. At one time the sanatorium was filled with rusting wheelchairs and dirty medical equipment, and the operating room was painted with old bloodstains. One woman who worked there when it was a mental hospital said all the staff and patients regularly heard screams in empty wards and shuffling in unoccupied beds, and these sounds still reverberate through the building today. Rumour has it that a nurse was murdered by a patient long ago, leaving her spirit to forever wander the grounds.

But the most frightening place on the property remains the dark tunnels that snake their way through the dirt below the town. People have heard voices and seen shadowy figures in these murky depths, as if the ghosts of the bodies that were once carted underground are still stuck six feet under.

Staff of Tranquille Farm — the new owners — recently made an unusual discovery during an investigation of the tunnels: near the morgue where the bodies were stored are a dining hall and a barbershop, giving new meaning to the expression "a hair-raising experience."

In Tranquille, you get two ghost towns for the price of one — one above ground, one below. Few have the guts to venture very deep into either, let alone both.

A GHOSTLY ALMA MATER

St. Thomas, Ontario

As mortified onlookers watched in horror and recorded the event on their mobile phones, the towering and iconic steeple of Alma College collapsed a little after noon on May 28, 2008. The grand, Gothic building had been engulfed in a raging inferno, the fire started by two teenage boys. Fortunately, no one was harmed in the fire as the college had sat vacant since it closed in 1988. But one has to wonder what became of the tormented souls that haunted the building after the blaze reduced it to cinders and ash.

The most well-known ghost of Alma College haunted its halls for nearly a century. It was an all-girls private school built in 1878 that focused its studies on literature, art and music, with a student body that included young women from around the globe.

Elissa Lyman, a student from 1983 to 1986, lived nearby and therefore didn't sleep in the dormitory like so many of her classmates. She recalls with unease the times when winter weather made it too dangerous to drive home after class, forcing her to spend the night. They were often restless, those nights spent in the dorm, as her sleep was plagued by the bizarre sounds that filled the school. The only explanation Elissa could think of for the midnight noises was that they were caused by the wanderings of Angela, the spirit the girls dubbed "the Ghost of Alma" in hushed tones.

The details surrounding Angela are a little hazy and stories vary, but a retired teacher confirmed that the faculty and staff reported seeing her ghost in the castle-like building as early as the 1930s. Most people believe that Angela was a music teacher, although some assert she was a house mother (someone assigned to ensure the young girls behaved appropriately and patrolled the halls after curfew). Regardless of Angela's position within Alma College, everyone agrees that she was a mean woman who was nasty toward the students, making her disliked by all.

Legend has it a group of teen girls decided to play a prank on Angela, hoping to give her a taste of her own medicine. They locked her in a cupboard and left her there overnight, but it's unlikely they intended for their "joke" to have such dire consequences. The cupboard was too small and sealed airtight, and Angela soon ran out of air. Her suffocated body was found the next morning.

Shortly thereafter, her ghost was seen in what was nicknamed the Ivory Tower, one of two stairwells leading to a storage room on the second floor at the south end of the building. Some have reported that if you stay alone in the Ivory Tower long enough you'll see her descending the stairs, and others not brave enough to attempt that feat have heard her footsteps walk past. It's a telling sign that the Ivory Tower's walls were unmarked while the second tower's walls were covered with the signatures of generations of schoolgirls. Apparently, no one wanted to deface the stairwell where Angela dwelt.

Many years after Alma College closed and began to fall into disrepair, a team of ghost hunters snuck onto the grounds and crept through the dust-covered halls. They slowly climbed the creaking stairs to the very top of the Ivory Tower. Here, one of the braver people in the group knocked on the wall. It was answered by the hollow sound of another knock.

"Is this Angela?" the ghost hunter asked.

"Yes," said a very low whisper.

As this was the very type of experience the group had hoped for, they didn't turn and run. They also noted that, despite Angela's reputation for having gone through life as a mean-spirited woman, her ghost did not give them a bad vibe. Perhaps she has remained on this plane to atone for her sins and to make up for the way she mistreated her young students. Perhaps she's a new woman, so to speak.

The peaceful feeling the group got from Angela, however, did not extend to the rest of the college. They constantly felt unwanted and surrounded by a dark, evil energy that they attributed to many ghosts, some old but most young. At first the spirits seemed merely curious about the intruders. On the main staircase voices called out, "Who are you?" and "Why are you here?" In the library the leader's hand was innocently grabbed by a small child. But the longer they remained, the more active — and upset — the spirits became.

In the basement they witnessed objects being moved on their own and heard a voice warn them to *leave now.* Unheeding the advice, the ghost hunters travelled up to the old dorm rooms where, if the story is to be believed, the girls who murdered Angela would have spent their nights. The visitors described the area as a hot spot for dark entities, all identifiable as teenage girls. The group used a digital recorder that, when played back, revealed so many voices overlapping each other that much of what was said couldn't be understood. But the words that cut through

Stairs leading to the main floor and basement

the ruckus were foul, abusive and threatening. Sticks and stones may break your bones, but so would a hard shove at the top of the stairs. And the dead girls repeatedly tried to trip and push the living intruders in this part of the building.

Today the grounds where Alma College once stood with pride are empty except for shattered bricks and burnt wood. Although you'll never be able to climb the Ivory Tower and ask Angela if she's still there, or brave the dangerously haunted dormitory, it's said that the ghosts of Alma College still linger amidst the rubble of the grandiose building. In this light, the college's motto is fitting:

Though we are far from thee
Still we long for thee
Ever loyal still

FED INTO THE FURNACE

Edmonton, Alberta

You might think that a gruesome murder story and a resident ghost might be bad for a hotel's business, but for La Bohème in Edmonton, the opposite is true. Every Halloween the building is booked to capacity with guests hoping to catch a glimpse of the spectre that has terrorized many people over the years.

Built in 1912, La Bohème was originally a luxury three-storey apartment building with shops on the main floor before being converted into a bed and breakfast in 1982. The story of the murder that happened while it was an apartment building is so horrific, so grisly, that the faint of heart might not want to read any further.

Still with me?

Don't say I didn't warn you.

As co-owner and caretaker Mike Comeau and his ghost-hunting guests will tell you, the legend goes like this: the original caretaker murdered his wife on the top floor of the building and dragged her body by the feet down three flights of stairs. Then, in the dark, dingy basement, he fed her corpse into the furnace. But in order to make it fit, he had to chop it up into tiny pieces.

Since that day people have had terrifying experiences in the building. Guests have been woken in the middle of the night by the *thud, thud, thud* sound of a head banging down the stairs, only to rush into the hallway, turn on a light and see . . . an empty staircase.

Larry Finnson, a businessman and regular guest at La Bohème, had a particularly scary experience one night. While staying in Suite 7, the most haunted room, he woke

Furnace of La Bohème

up to find his bed levitating in mid-air.

The murdered woman's ghost has also bothered employees of the bed and breakfast. One woman was alone doing laundry in the basement next to the furnace room when she was suddenly grabbed from behind. Comeau says she was so petrified that she ran screaming up the stairs and straight out the front door, never to return.

Have a flip through La Bohème's guest book and you'll find otherworldly accounts forever etched in history by the hotel's visitors, such as the couple who saw a beautiful woman in their closet at night, a woman whose feet had been severed from her legs.

Given the claims of what a previous caretaker used it for, you might be surprised to learn that the original furnace is still being used to heat the building today. If you visit La Bohème it'll keep you warm through the night, even when your blood turns to ice.

DINING WITH THE DEAD

Halifax, Nova Scotia

Standing proudly on the busy downtown corner of Carmichael and Argyle Streets, the Five Fishermen Restaurant is one of Halifax's busiest dining locations. But it's not only bustling during open hours — some customers don't wish to leave after it closes for the night. These customers don't require much service from the wait staff. You see, they don't eat anything and have a habit of disappearing into thin air when approached.

The brick-and-wood building was built in 1817 as a schoolhouse before becoming the Halifax Victorian School of Art. The school was run by Anna Leonowens in the years after she served as governess to the children of the King of Siam, which was made famous in the musical film *The King and I*. Despite this claim to fame, the school closed in the late 1800s and the building became even more famous — or rather, *infamous.*

In 1883 the building was converted into the John Snow & Co. Funeral Home, setting the stage for its morbid destiny.

On April 14, 1912, the RMS *Titanic* struck an iceberg during its maiden voyage from the United Kingdom to New York City. It sank a little less than three hours later in the North Atlantic Ocean, six hundred kilometres south of Newfoundland. It was the largest ship afloat at the time and its passengers were some of the wealthiest in the world. The sinking of the RMS *Titanic* was one of the deadliest maritime disasters in modern history, claiming the lives of more than fifteen hundred passengers. As the nearest mainland port, Halifax served as the home base for the rescue operations, and most of the bodies were brought to John Snow & Co. Funeral Home.

Five short years later, still reeling from the shock of the *Titanic's* sinking, Nova Scotia was dealt another tragedy of unfathomable magnitude: the Halifax explosion. On December 6, 1917, a French cargo ship loaded with wartime explosives struck a second ship near Halifax Harbour. Twenty minutes later a fire ignited the cargo, creating the largest man-made explosion prior to the creation of nuclear weapons. The blast decimated an entire district of downtown Halifax, and flying debris, collapsing buildings and fires killed approximately two thousand people and injured nine thousand others. Once again, many of the dead were taken to the John Snow & Co. Funeral Home.

Having served as the final destination for so many victims of two of the modern world's greatest disasters, it's no wonder many people are struck by an unexplainable energy as soon as they set foot inside. But after the building changed hands once again and opened as the Five Fishermen Restaurant in 1975, customers unaware of the history might not be expecting a side of fright with their foie gras.

The spooky stories restaurant employees have shared are so numerous that they could nearly fill an entire book on their own. The staff are so accustomed to the spirits they work with that they no longer bat an eye when glasses fly from shelves, water taps turn on and off or cutlery lifts off tables and crashes on the floor. It's common for the staff to hear their names whispered in their ears when they're all alone. One employee once rushed into a private room called the Captain's Quarters because he heard a man and a woman arguing, only to find the room empty. Servers have seen a misty grey apparition float down the stairs to the kitchen as they were closing the restaurant. Even more disconcerting was the time a server heard a tapping sound upon a second floor window, which was especially odd since nothing on ground level could reach the window. When she approached to investigate, she saw the same misty grey apparition hovering outside in the air.

Then there's the man, old and tall with long grey hair, dressed in a black greatcoat from another time. He's been spotted a few times, most notably by a young man whose task it was to prepare the salad bar before the dinner rush. One warm summer day he was carrying crates of vegetables to the bar when he heard a loud crash nearby. Unsure what could have caused the commotion — he was alone in the restaurant at the time — he set the vegetables down and wandered around the dining area. On the floor he found a shattered ashtray, which he knelt down to examine. When he stood back up he happened to look in a mirror, and in it he saw the old man in the long black coat walking toward him from behind. The young man dropped the ashtray and spun around, but the grey-haired man had disappeared.

You might have noticed that a common thread running through these stories is that the paranormal activity only occurs when there aren't any customers in the restaurant, but that's not always the case.

One evening a group of diners tried to send a text message from their table, but only one word — which the diners hadn't typed — was sent to the recipient of the message: DEATH.

John Snow & Co., second building from right, with coffins for victims of the Halifax explosion stacked outside

Another particularly busy night, the hostess was walking a couple to their table. As they crossed the dining room she suddenly felt something hit her across the face, but she couldn't detect the cause, so she assumed it was her imagination. After seating the couple, the hostess returned to the restaurant's entrance where the maître d' looked at her gravely and asked in a hushed tone, "What happened to your face?"

There, across the hostess's cheek, as if she'd been slapped, was an angry red handprint.

WHERE HORROR AND HOCKEY SHARE A HOME

Toronto, Ontario

One bright and cheery summer day, a young boy toured the Hockey Hall of Fame with a group of adults. Like the three hundred thousand people who visit every year, the boy enjoyed the displays featuring Maurice "The Rocket" Richard and Wayne Gretzky, tested his own skills in the NHLPA Be a Player Zone and marvelled at the Stanley Cup up close.

Suddenly, as he passed through one of the exhibits, the boy stopped dead in his tracks. His rigid stance and wide eyes were so odd and out of place that the adults wondered what could possibly be wrong with him. Then, with a trembling hand, he pointed at an empty wall.

"What is it?" they asked him.

"Don't you see her?" he screamed over and over and over.

"Don't you see her? Don't you see her? Don't you see her?"

There was no one there. "See who?" they asked fearfully.

Jane Rodney, who was the Hall's coordinator of resource centre services at the time, says the boy saw a woman with long black hair pass back and forth through the wall as if daring him to look away.

The description matched that of Dorothea "Dorothy" Mae Elliott, the Hockey Hall of Fame's resident ghost. The boy is only one of two people who have seen Dorothy's ghost, but plenty of others have had terrifying experiences and witnessed paranormal activity in the building since 1953. That was the year Dorothy died in the women's washroom from a self-inflicted gunshot wound.

Before the Hockey Hall of Fame opened in 1993, the grand building that stands out among the contemporary skyscrapers was a branch of the Bank of Montreal for nearly one hundred years. Dorothy was a bank teller and, by her co-workers' accounts, she was beautiful, sociable and very popular. But it was whispered around the bank that she was harbouring a dark secret. It was believed she was having an affair with a married man, either another teller or one of the branch managers. Perhaps this transgression is what led her to take her own life.

Co-worker Doreen Bracken arrived on the fateful day at 8:00 a.m. and was surprised to find Dorothy already at work looking tired, unkempt and depressed. At 9:00 a.m. another employee began screaming over the balcony of the second floor. Doreen and others raced upstairs and found Dorothy on the floor of the women's washroom, a puddle of blood quickly spreading across the floor. Beside her body was the bank's revolver, a .38 calibre that tellers were expected to use in case of a robbery.

Shortly thereafter signs of Dorothy's lingering spirit were witnessed by the staff. The women refused to use the second floor washroom. They felt a presence within, an unpleasant one, like they were being watched. Management finally gave in and had a new washroom built in the basement, but unexplainable occurrences persisted. Lights flickered on and off. Objects disappeared and reappeared mysteriously.

Korea, 55,000 Canadian troops have served overseas and form a valuable reserve force in case of emergency. When Korea began we had six major military units, now we have 26, he said. "Even with what we now call slippages, it has been possible to adhere closely to our original plan."

GIRL BANK CLERK, 19 DIES OF GUN WOUND

A 19-year-old clerk of the Bank of Montreal, Yonge and Front Sts., died today in St. Michael's hospital of a self-inflicted revolver wound in her head. Death came 22 hours after she was found in the washroom of the bank. Doctors were amazed she had lived so long.

The attractive girl, who lived with her married sister on Burnhamthorpe Rd., Islington, is believed by police to have been lonesome for her boy friend who left during the week-end to take a job on the boats.

Entering the office early, she was "kidded," police said, by other employees about getting in so early. She shrugged her shoulders and smiled, then walked over to the messenger's desk. Without being seen, she took the revolver and went to the washroom where she was found a short time later.

DYCE AGAIN PRESIDENT

P.C. Alex Dyce was re-elected president of the Toronto Police War Veteran's association last night. Other officers named were: P.C. John Colclough, first vice-president; Det. John Crilly, second vice-president; P.C. Ray Ryan, secretary, and P.C. Jack Beer, treasurer.

It's amazing—es whiter with than any soap product know wash water, no blueing, no b freshly-rinsed than you can g cause Fab wash dulling soap sc

FAST DIS **HALF T**

Sparkling dishes without wiping! New Impr through g can! No

A notice appearing in the Toronto Daily Star on March 13, 1953

Locked doors and windows suddenly flew open of their own accord.

Custodial workers have had some of the most frightening experiences while working alone through the night. When all is dark and quiet, footsteps creak along the floorboards overhead, moans and shrieks echo from the second floor and some have even felt phantom hands grab and push them from behind.

Rob Hynes, who was previously the Hockey Hall of Fame special events supervisor, witnessed something he'll never forget. He was in the building early one morning preparing for an event. Suddenly he had the unusual feeling that someone was watching him. The odd sensation drew him into a pitch-black room on the second floor where the sensation was the strongest. What happened inside the room was unexpected and terrifying. A chair was spinning in circles as if caught in the middle of a small cyclone. Suddenly the chair slid across the floor and right into his hand. Despite the fact that Hynes is skeptical when it comes to ghosts, he wasted no time fleeing the room.

Other than the young boy, the other person who saw Dorothy's ghost in the metaphorical flesh is Joanna Jordan, a Toronto musician. She was commissioned to play the harp in the Great Hall during an event. She was unaware that the building had a haunted history, so she wasn't prepared at all when she looked up and saw Dorothy's ghost floating just below the second floor ceiling, looking down upon her intently. To this day the image of the black-haired woman staring at her from the ceiling is as vivid in Joanna's memory as on the day she saw Dorothy. She returned to the building a few years later but, try as she might, she couldn't head up to the second floor.

Our country's national sport can be a hard-hitting, aggressive game filled with fights, body checks, bruisers and goons. It's fitting that the Hockey Hall of Fame is home to a presence more chilling than a few hours spent outdoors playing pond hockey in the middle of January.

THE BOY IN THE BASEMENT

New Westminster, British Columbia

A school is supposed to be a place for learning, a place where children feel safe, a place to grow. It's not supposed to be a place where a boy in the basement relives his death over and over.

But then New Westminster Secondary School has a morbid history dating back to its construction. The site where the school now sits was used in the mid to late 1800s as a cemetery for marginalized groups of the day, including Chinese pioneers, Aboriginal people, convicted criminals and the mentally handicapped. The school was built in 1949, and the cemetery was found when a bulldozer unearthed an unmarked coffin. But nothing was done about the ghastly discovery, and construction of the school continued.

Today the school has a good reputation for its academic program and is one of the largest high schools in British Columbia. It also has an abundance of athletic facilities, including four gyms, a football field, two soccer fields, a skating rink, a fitness room and a skateboard park. But some people contest whether there was ever a swimming pool. Some say the pool was in the basement when the school first opened but it's since been filled in with concrete. Others believe the pool only exists as part of the school's lore. Regardless of what New Westminster residents believe, one thing most of the school's alumni can agree on is that the building has a creepy vibe, particularly in the basement.

The reports claim that a male student drowned in the pool in the early 1970s and that it was filled in years later due to safety concerns. In the time between the drowning and the pool's closure, however, security guards regularly saw a boy floating face down in the water during their nightly rounds. They would turn to grab a pole or call for help, but when they turned back the boy would be gone and the water perfectly still. These reports from the guards seem to support the existence of the pool at one time in the school's history.

Guards have also reported similar paranormal activity in the archery range, also located in the basement. A man is said to have been seen firing a phantom bow and arrows, only to disappear when anyone got too close.

Another male student is said to have died in the 1980s in the school's woodworking shop, which, unlike the pool, is definitely still in operation today. No one has reported coming face to face with the woodworking boy, but he has been spotted by night guards on the security camera monitors. When they run to the room, the boy is gone.

Even the music room isn't immune to paranormal activity, as the school's cameras have also picked up unexplained glowing orbs hovering in the air.

Just like the existence of the pool in the basement, some people believe that the reports of the deaths in the school have been fabricated. If they're right, it's possible that all the ghostly sightings in New Westminster Secondary School over the years can be attributed to the bones that unceremoniously clog the dirt beneath the building's foundation.

THE LADY IN BLUE

Peggy's Cove, Nova Scotia

The ocean is known for its mesmerizing beauty that's as dangerous as it is breathtaking. It's widely believed among ghost enthusiasts that a soul who perishes in the water is likely to meet such a traumatic end that he or she has a difficult time moving on and finding peace. When that soul willingly drowns in the deep blue, committing suicide, the likelihood of a haunting is even greater. A legend from one of Atlantic Canada's most popular tourist destinations confirms this belief.

Located forty-four kilometres southwest of Halifax, Peggy's Cove is a small fishing village known for its photographic beauty, quaint homes and the Peggy's Point Lighthouse, one of Canada's most iconic images. Strict land-use laws have maintained the idyllic atmosphere of Peggy's Cove, preventing rapid property development and keeping the population to a mere six hundred people. Although the inhabitants still fish for lobster, tourism has become more economically important to the community than fishing. The tourists come to see the boats, the lobster traps and the famous lighthouse, but many are confronted by something they hadn't planned on seeing: The Lady in Blue, an ethereal spirit that walks the shoreline. She's such a sad vision that it might chill your heart and make your blood run cold simply to look at her.

A few legends have popped up to explain her existence. The most popular is that a woman named Margaret lived in the area in the 1700s before it was called Peggy's Cove. The source of the name of the village isn't documented, so some believe it comes from nearby Saint Margaret's Bay ("Peggy" is a nickname of Margaret), which Samuel de Champlain named after his mother, Marguerite. But others believe that it's named after Margaret, The Lady in Blue. It's said she was the sole survivor of a shipwreck in 1800, a disaster that claimed the lives of everyone onboard, including her young children, but spared her. She'd walk the shores for days on end, her blue dress rippling in the wind and her eyes scanning the Atlantic Ocean. Little did Margaret know that, while she watched the water, Death was watching her.

Her second husband, in an attempt to cure his wife's depression, joined her one day on the rocky shore. He stepped in front of her and danced a jig, hoping to amuse Margaret, maybe even make her smile or laugh. But his

The lighthouse at Peggy's Cove

foot slipped, he fell, his head cracked against the rocks and he died a quick, bloody death.

The grief from back-to-back tragedies was too much for poor Margaret to bear. She was seen one day shortly after the death of her husband walking into the ocean . . . and was never seen again.

Well, not *alive.*

The ghost of Margaret — or Peggy of the Cove, as she's become known — has become a permanent resident of the small fishing village. Since the lighthouse was built in 1868, The Lady in Blue has been spotted forever wandering the rocky shores at its base. Some say she looks like she's about to jump into the Atlantic, others claim she's spoken softly to them, but everyone agrees: she's not a threatening or frightening ghost, but a deeply sad one. Like the relentless crash of cool blue waves upon the shore, Margaret's soul will never give up the search for the family she lost.

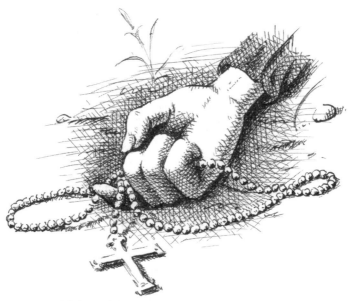

THE HAUNTED HOTEL

Victoria, British Columbia

Spend a night in The Fairmont Empress Hotel and chances are you won't be spending the night alone. Unexpected guests — the type of guests who can pass *through* doors instead of needing to open them — have a habit of haunting the halls and bedrooms in this grand hotel.

With nearly five hundred rooms and an imposing presence overlooking Victoria's Inner Harbour, The Empress is one of the oldest and most famous hotels in British Columbia. Since it opened in 1908 it has welcomed kings, queens, movie stars and other notable celebrities, including *The Jungle Book* author Rudyard Kipling. It's little wonder some souls never want to leave, even after all earthly ties have been severed from their bodies.

A carpenter is likely the ghost that's been haunting The

Empress for the longest time. It's said the worker hanged himself from the rafters of the west wing during the hotel's construction, two years before it opened. For as long as The Empress has been open to the public, countless guests have reported seeing a man with bulging eyes and a thick rope cutting into his neck swaying from the roof. It's not known why the carpenter committed suicide, but if you pass through the West Wing late at night, don't look up — you might not like what you see.

The carpenter has been hanging out in the hotel for a little longer than the spirit of Lizzie McGrath, a chambermaid who worked and lived in the hotel when it opened. She lived in a room on the sixth floor, which used to be designated for chambermaids. Lizzie was a devout Irish Catholic and by all accounts a hard worker. She had a habit of stepping out of her room and onto the fire escape after a long, arduous day cleaning The Empress's many guest rooms. Under the pale glow of the moon, she'd clear her head and complete her rosary. The night air revitalized her body and her faith, giving her peace. In 1909, when the first addition was being added to the hotel, the fire escapes were removed so they wouldn't be in the way of construction. But no one told poor Lizzie. Unbeknownst to her, she completed what would be her final (living) day of work, returned to her room, grabbed her rosary beads and stepped outside, falling six storeys to her death. Construction workers rolled her body over early the next morning. Clutched tightly in her hands were her beloved rosary beads.

Lizzie's hard-working attitude has extended into the

The Fairmont Empress Hotel

afterlife, and her ghost is often seen on the sixth floor, still carrying out her cleaning duties.

At least Lizzie's spirit seems to be at home, so to speak. The ghost of another woman stuck in The Empress isn't so lucky. Many guests have been awoken by loud, frantic pounding on their doors in the middle of the night. In the hall, panicked and disoriented, is a lost woman in pajamas who pleads for help. Leading guests by her icy-cold hand, she takes them to the elevator . . . and then simply disappears. It's believed she used to haunt a room that was demolished to build a new elevator and is now left to wander the hotel's halls, forever looking for her room, forever lost.

But the hotel's most famous ghost is its architect, Francis Rattenbury, whose final days were mired in controversy. Following the opening of The Empress, Rattenbury became a well-known and respected public figure in Victoria, but he tarnished his reputation when he left his wife and children to marry a woman, Alma, who was less than half his age. Following a string of bad investments and the stress of the scandal, Rattenbury was murdered in his drawing-room in England, his skull cracked open by either a carpenter's hammer or croquet mallet (the reports of the weapon vary). His chauffeur, George, was charged and convicted of the murder, and it was revealed that George and Alma had been a secret couple for some time. Shortly after Rattenbury was murdered, Alma took her own life, stabbing a knife into her broken heart.

Rattenbury, it would appear, wishes to remain in the hotel he designed, reliving his glory days before he made a string of poor choices that ultimately led to his untimely death. He wanders The Empress's halls, keeping an eye on his crowning achievement and its many guests — many of whom are, like Rattenbury, long since deceased.

THE HANGMAN'S KNOT

Quebec City, Quebec

Place Royale is not only a beautifully quaint and historic square in the heart of Old Quebec, it's also considered to be the birthplace of New France. Founded in 1608 by French navigator and explorer Samuel de Champlain, the area first served as a bustling fur marketplace and is home to Notre-Dame-des-Victoires, the oldest stone church in North America. But behind the charming facade of the heritage buildings and cobblestone streets lies a violent past that has ensnared its fair share of spirits.

Today, Place Royale is a must-see destination for tourists, many of whom step off one of the many cruise ships that dock in nearby Old Port for a little sightseeing. But even travellers desperate to stretch their legs after a long sea voyage might not spend too long on land before hurrying back to their ships after nightfall. The man in the shadows who watches all who pass through Place Royale's gates and the woman who hauntingly roams around the Notre-Dame-des-Victoires church each and every night are neither tourists nor locals. Well, they're not locals to *present*-day Place Royale, seeing as they were both killed in the 1600s.

In addition to the hustle and bustle of the trading that took place in the market square, Place Royale was also where men, women and children found guilty of crimes were executed in brutal fashion. And even those found guilty of minor crimes were given a one-way ticket to visit the hangman, including the very first person executed in Quebec City: a 16-year-old girl charged with petty theft.

One short month after Champlain established Place Royale, he caught wind of a plot to murder him. He received a covert report that four men, led by locksmith Jean Duval, planned to deliver the slain Champlain and Quebec into the hands of the Spanish for their own profit. Armed with this information, Champlain struck first and invited the four men to his house for dinner. Thinking it would be the perfect opportunity to complete their murderous plan, Duval and the others accepted the invitation and arrived at his doorstep. But before they could harm Champlain, he had them arrested for treason. The three followers were sent to France to be executed, but Champlain had a special plan for their ringleader. Duval was hanged beside Place Royale's gate, but that wasn't enough to deter copycats. Duval's lifeless body was then beheaded before the crowd. His head was deposited on a pike and placed atop

Notre-Dame-des-Victoires

the highest rooftop. His blank stare upon the square below served as a constant warning against treason. His ghost — a shadowy figure spotted by many tourists after nightfall — has taken up permanent residence near the gate where his body once swayed at the end of a rope.

If it's any consolation for the ghost of Duval, he's had

another executed criminal's spirit to keep him company in Place Royale. In 1680, not long after Duval was hanged and decapitated, a new executioner was appointed. Jean Gatier was advised to move with his wife and small children out of the city so that he wouldn't live amongst the very people he might one day need to kill. He did so willingly, never imagining that, regardless of how far he lived from the city limits, he would still be living with someone he would one day execute.

Shortly after they moved far from Place Royale, his wife was convicted of stealing goods from a merchant. Her sentence was death by hanging. The executioner was forced to do the heartbreaking task, hanging his own wife and the mother of his children in front of Notre-Dame-des-Victoires church. The apparition of Madame Gatier still wanders the cobblestone alleyways in Place Royale, eternally searching for her husband. Whether she pines for a reunion or revenge is unknown.

THE WATER GHOST

Holland Cove, Prince Edward Island

Prince Edward Island is well known as the setting of Lucy Maud Montgomery's beloved *Anne of Green Gables*. The beauty of P.E.I.'s rolling green hills and red, sandy beaches set the perfect stage for Montgomery's stories, which are worldwide bestsellers. It's fitting that a province known around the globe for its idyllic "island life" would be the home of a waterlogged ghost that rises with the tide.

Each year on July 14, when the tide is at its highest point, inhabitants of Holland Cove report seeing a woman appear from the murky depths of the water. She's dressed in a white gown and her long black hair hangs heavily from her scalp. Once on land she leaves a wet trail in her wake that never stops flowing from her body. She wanders up and down the beach, her wet eyes filled with sadness, and calls, "Samuel? Samuel?" Never finding the man she seeks, she eventually wanders back into the water to drown herself. Year after year she resurfaces, searches in vain for Samuel, then commits her body to the waves once more. Year after year no body is ever recovered from the surf.

Who is she, and who is Samuel? These are questions that all who have come face to face with the water ghost have asked themselves for a long, long time. Most believe the man she's in search of is none other than Captain Samuel Johannes Holland, the namesake of Holland Cove. Appointed Surveyor General of North America by the British, Captain Holland came to the area in 1764 and spent the next two years creating detailed maps that are still in use today. Captain Holland fell in love with Canada

Holland Cove

and spent the rest of his days here before his death in 1801.

The legend states that the ghost is Captain Holland's wife, a beautiful woman named Racine who came from French royalty. One wintry day on the cove, Captain Holland was late returning home from an expedition. Fearing the worst, Racine carelessly ventured out onto the ice in hopes of seeing her husband, but the ice was too thin and it cracked. Racine plummeted into the icy water and drowned. Captain Holland returned shortly thereafter to the heartbreaking news, but it wasn't long before he was reunited with his deceased bride. He reported seeing her a few days later, soaked to the bone and deathly pale, wailing and calling his name, before vanishing in front of his very eyes.

The story doesn't hold much water due to some large holes. First, the ghost appears every summer, but Racine supposedly died in the winter — it's common lore for ghosts to appear on the date of their death. Some believe this can be explained by the high tide, which might spew her spirit to the beach much like a piece of driftwood.

The larger problem is that Captain Holland was married twice but neither wife was named Racine. His second wife, the one who lived with him at Holland Cove, Marie-Joseph Rollet, was French as the legend suggests. It's possible "Racine" was a nickname. However, Marie-Joseph outlived her husband, so it's unlikely the ghost can be attributed to her if the story is to be believed.

The true identity of the water ghost might never be determined, but that won't stop the tide from rising. Every July the water ghost is sure to emerge from the ocean, water draining from her every pore as she laments the loss of Samuel. And whether or not you believe in the legend of Racine and Captain Holland, you'd be well advised to heed one piece of advice those familiar with the tale hasten to add: if you hear the water ghost of Holland Cove, don't venture anywhere near her. It's believed everyone who lays eyes on her will one day drown as well.

DEAD AND BURIED, BUT NOT GONE

St. John's, Newfoundland and Labrador

Some buildings inspire fear the moment you spot them. Others are trickier and don't immediately stand out, like they're trying to hide a secret or erase the past. One such location is the Cathedral Street Bistro in downtown St. John's. On the surface it's a charming restaurant offering fine dining, a small red building attached to a larger blue one that was at one time rented out for use as apartments. But appearances can be deceiving, and the stories about the Cathedral Street Bistro point to the building's eerie, hidden history.

A number of businesses were located in the building before the Cathedral Street Bistro opened, including other restaurants, an inn and the aforementioned apartments. But it also used to be a funeral home dating back to 1891, the final earthly stop for many a soul, and many believe the ghosts that still dwell within the restaurant date back to that time. Some even believe the negative energy of the living people who visited the funeral home to grieve the loss of a loved one is soaked into the walls like a stain that can't be washed clean. Whatever one decides to believe, there's no question that the stories told in hushed tones about the Cathedral Street Bistro are frightening.

Brian Abbott owned and operated Chez Briann, one of the restaurants that occupied the building before the Cathedral Street Bistro opened. He knows of at least two spirits that have haunted its halls. One day an employee began to walk down the stairs when she saw something and stopped. There was a person at the bottom of the staircase, but the figure appeared to be made more of smoke than flesh and bone. Suddenly the misty spectre flew up the stairs and passed straight through her.

The other ghost his staff encountered regularly was an old man who dwelled in the dining room when the restaurant was quiet. He had a stern face and ice-cold eyes, and would catch your stare as if challenging you to look away or run. That's exactly what the wait staff would do. For every time they held his stare for more than a few seconds he would begin to approach them. No one ever stuck around long enough to discover the stern man's intentions.

It's certainly not the type of place you'd want to spend the night, but of course, that's exactly what people did when the building was the Victoria Station Inn during the 1990s. One night a woman woke up with severe pain in her chest. Floating above her was a ghost, an old man, quite possibly the same one that would later be seen by restaurant staff. She lay paralyzed in her bed, unable to blink and forced to watch as the man placed two coins over her eyes. The act of placing two coins on a dead body's eyelids is an old custom based on the belief that the departed would need the money to pay a boatman to carry the body across the river Styx. But this woman was still alive. Either the man was mistaken or his actions hinted at darker plans. Fortunately, the woman regained control of her body and was able to escape before the ghost could harm her.

Others have reported seeing a lost spirit, this time a woman, wandering the halls in the middle of the night. She doesn't speak or approach anyone, but those who have gotten close enough have seen a distinguishing characteristic that never fails to chill the blood: running down the length of her torso is a jagged scar, as if from a recent autopsy.

It's unsettling to think that, as guests wine and dine in the restaurant, it's still business as usual for the funeral home that closed its doors long ago. But the spirits of those who worked there or were prepared for burial within have no intention of going quietly into the night.

VALLEY OF THE HEADLESS MEN

Nahanni National Park Reserve, Northwest Territories

The Nahanni National Park Reserve, approximately five hundred kilometres west of Yellowknife, is a sprawling land filled with breathtaking scenery, endangered wildlife and a dark, deadly past. Although it's only accessible by boat or plane, one thousand adventurous souls brave the elements each year to witness first-hand the isolating power of the park. Caution must be exercised — history has proven that it's all too easy to lose one's way, or worse, one's head, in the Nahanni.

A UNESCO World Heritage site, Nahanni National Park is filled with steaming geysers, vicious sinkholes, icy caverns and a waterfall nearly twice as high as Niagara Falls. But in the early 1900s it wasn't the scenery that attracted people to the location, but the mad hope that gold was nestled in the hills. Rumours began to swirl that two brothers, Willie and Frank McLeod, had staked a claim. Even if that were true it did them little good. In 1908, after a year without word from either brother, their bodies were found next to a Nahanni river. Their heads were not.

In the years that followed, more bodies — each roughly a foot shorter than they should have been — kept piling up.

In 1917, Swiss prospector Martin Jorgenson was found very close to the river where the McLeod brothers' bodies were discovered. Jorgenson, likewise, had been decapitated. Shortly thereafter a trapper named John O'Brien lost his head to an unknown assailant. And in 1945 an Ontario miner was found in his sleeping bag with his head severed from his shoulders.

These mysterious and gruesome murders have given the 200 Mile Gorge area the brutally honest nickname "Valley of the Headless Men." Take a glance at a map and you'll find other morbidly named locations such as Deadman Valley, Headless Creek, Headless Range and Funeral Range. It's as if the people who named these spots wished to warn visitors of the horror they might encounter in the park.

Odd occurrences and unexplained mysteries in the remote northern woodlands of the Nahanni, however, date much further back than the decapitation of the McLeods. There is evidence in the park of prehistoric human life dating back ten thousand years. A story passed down from generation to generation tells of a people known as the Naha. They were regarded by other tribes as a vicious group of thugs who would swarm down the great rivers and take advantage of all who lived in the lowlands. Eventually the lowland tribes decided to strike back, but when they travelled north and came across the Naha settlement, the fires had been put out and the tepees were empty. The Naha had vanished into thin air, never to be seen or heard from again.

Some attribute the disappearance of the Naha and the recent beheadings to the Nuk-Luk, a Sasquatch-like creature that has been spotted in the park. The Nuk-Luk is thought to have inhabited these woods for more than three thousand years, and at four hundred pounds and eight feet tall, he's a creature better left alone. Others attribute the deaths and disappearances to an evil — but unknown — entity that has long terrorized the Valley of the Headless Men. The surrounding indigenous people have steered clear of the area for many years, believing it to be haunted.

Big, strong outdoorsmen such as miners and trappers have been decapitated with ease. An entire people has been wiped out without a trace. No matter who (or what) is responsible for these mysteries, it's strongly encouraged that you keep a level head when you visit the Nahanni. Or else you might not keep your head at all.

EPILOGUE

Still don't believe in ghosts? Then maybe you should spend a night — alone — in a haunted house. That's what I decided to do while writing the book you hold in your hands. Throughout my research I was astounded by the credibility of the ghost stories I unearthed, by the sheer number of eyewitness accounts that lined up with one another, by the ability of the tales to get under my skin and send me running around my darkened home turning on every single light.

I had never seen a ghost myself. Don't ask me why (morbid curiosity, most likely), but I wanted to — *needed* to — change that.

And so I drove to the picturesque town of Niagara-on-the-Lake and checked into The Olde Angel Inn. You know an inn is old when it spells the word with an E. In fact, it's the oldest inn in Ontario, incorporated in 1789. It burned down (and was later rebuilt) after the War of 1812. It's a beautiful building that has sheltered many famous guests over the years, including the first Lieutenant-Governor of Upper Canada, John Graves Simcoe; explorer Alexander Mackenzie; and Queen Victoria's father, Prince Edward. In short, it's seen a lot of history, and some of that history has been bloody.

Naturally, The Olde Angel Inn has a resident ghost.

During a secret rendezvous at the inn with his sweetheart, Captain Colin Swayze of the British Army hid in the cellar when he received word that American soldiers had invaded the town. He slipped into a barrel and hoped he'd go undetected. He didn't. The Americans stormed the inn, thundered down the cellar steps and stabbed each of the barrels with their bayonets. Captain Swayze spent his final living moments alone and afraid as he watched the blood drain from his body.

Shortly after the captain's death, people began witnessing odd things, and reports of paranormal activity continue to this day. Items fly off shelves. Footsteps plod down empty halls. A man in an old-fashioned military uniform walks through rooms in the middle of the night without pausing to open doors.

After interviewing staff and being guided into the cramped cellar to see the exact spot where Captain Swayze was killed, I spent a night in the General's Quarters, the Angel's most haunted bedroom. I locked myself in (little good that would do), left the lights on and pulled the bedsheet up to my chin.

Unexplained noises filled the room throughout the night. Out of the corner of my eye I saw countless shadows moving about. A curtain rustled as if someone hid behind it. My room key, dangling over the edge of a small table in the corner of the room where most of the paranormal activity has been witnessed, swayed from side to side on its own — I checked for a draft or an open window but the air around the key was dead still. A toy rabbit my daughter had lent me rested on the floor facing my bed as I finally fell into a restless sleep. When

I woke up, the rabbit was in the exact same spot . . . but had turned 180 degrees to face the wall.

I'm not exaggerating when I say I've never been so creeped out in my life. The goosebumps on my arms could've been used to sand wood.

Don't believe me? I had a feeling you might say that. So I decided to record the entire night with my camcorder. You can watch the video of my night alone in the haunted Olde Angel Inn on Scholastic Canada's website at www.scholastic.ca/hauntedcanada.

But before you visit the website and press play, make sure the lights are on. Grab a friend or sibling for safety in numbers. Make sure there's nothing under the bed or in the deepest corners of your closet, just in case.

And beware toy rabbits.

HAUNTED CANADA

Read the whole chilling series.

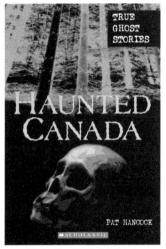

978-0-7791-1410-8

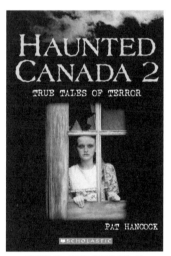

978-0-439-96122-6

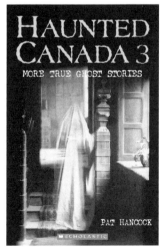

978-0-439-93777-1

978-0-545-99314-2

978-0-439-93875-4

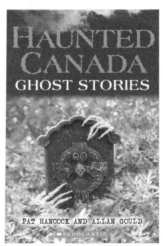

978-1-4431-2894-0

For Haunted Canada bonus material,
visit www.scholastic.ca/hauntedcanada.

Joel A. Sutherland is an author and librarian. He is the author of *Be a Writing Superstar* and *Frozen Blood*, a horror novel that was nominated for the Bram Stoker Award. His short fiction has appeared in many anthologies and magazines, including *Blood Lite II & III* and *Cemetery Dance* magazine, alongside the likes of Stephen King and Neil Gaiman. He is a two-time juror for the John Spray Mystery Award.

He appeared as "The Barbarian Librarian" on the Canadian edition of the hit television show ""' making it all the way to the third rour that librarians can be just as tougʰ one else. He has a Masters of I Studies from Aberystwyth Univε

Joel lives with his family in where he is still on the lookout fo.